THE EXILE OF TIME

TIME

By
RAY CUMMINGS

I0541404

ARMCHAIR FICTION
PO Box 4369, Medford, Oregon   97501-0168

*For more information about Armchair Books and products, visit our
website at…*

www.armchairfiction.com

Or email us at…

armchairfiction@yahoo.com

SHE CAME FROM A DIFFERENT TIME

She screamed for help from behind a foggy pane of glass. George Rankin and Larry Gregory, being typical chivalrous men from 1935, threw a brick through the window and rescued the young damsel. She was a beautiful woman with an incredible story. She said she was a kidnap victim from the year 1777! But was she simply insane, or was she truly the victim of an amazing time-spanning scheme? Then, from somewhere out of Time came a swarm of Robots that inflicted on New York City the awful vengeance of a diabolical cripple named Tugh. It was clear that an insidious plot was afoot that reached into the present day, as well as the unknown cities of the far-off future.

THE EXILE OF TIME is a tremendous tale of scientific wonders and nail-biting excitement, written by one of the true masters of 20th Century science fiction, Ray Cummings.

ABOUT RAY CUMMINGS...

Born in New York City in 1887, sci-fi great Ray Cummings' writings showed great insight into the limitless possibilities of future science. Much of this grew out of Cummings' personal relationship with American genius, Thomas Alva Edison.

During the 1920's and 1930's Cummings mesmerized thousands of readers with his amazing tales of time, other dimensions, and outer space. Tales like *Girl in the Golden Atom*, *Brigands of the Moon*, and *Wandl the Invader* established Cummings as a genre writer of the first magnitude. His imagination supplied a great many of the most common motifs that current science fiction holds dear, even to this day. While he followed in the tradition of other greats like Jules Verne and H. G. Wells, he also bridged the gap between those early masters and a newer style of sci-fi and fantasy writing that exploded into the field in the early and then the middle decades of the Twentieth Century.

When Ray Cummings passed on in January of 1957, the world of modern science fiction lost one of its true founding fathers.

Presently there was not one Robot, but three!

CHAPTER ONE
Mysterious Girl

THE extraordinary incidents began about 1 A.M. in the night of June 8-9, 1935. I was walking through Patton Place, in New York City, with my friend Larry Gregory. My name is George Rankin. My business—and Larry's—are details quite unimportant to this narrative. We had been friends in college. Both of us were working in New York; and with all our relatives in the middle west we were sharing an apartment on this Patton Place—a short crooked, little-known street of not particularly impressive residential buildings lying near the section known as Greenwich Village, where towering office buildings of the business districts encroach close upon it.

This night at 1 A. M. it was deserted. A taxi stood at a corner; its chauffeur had left it there, and evidently gone to a nearby lunch room. The street lights were, as always, inadequate. The night was sultry and dark, with a leaden sky and a breathless humidity that presaged a thunder storm. The houses were mostly unlighted at this hour. There was an occasional apartment house among them, but mostly they were low, ramshackle affairs of brick and stone.

We were still three blocks from our apartment when without warning the incidents began which were to plunge us and all the city into disaster. We were upon the threshold of a mystery weird and strange, but we did not know it. Mysterious portals were swinging to engulf us. And all unknowing, we walked into them.

Larry was saying, "Wish we would get a storm to clear this air—*what the devil?* George, did you hear that?"

WE stood listening. There had sounded a choking, muffled scream. We were midway in the block. There was not a pedestrian in sight, nor any vehicle save the abandoned taxi at the corner.

"A woman," he said. "Did it come from this house?"

We were standing before a three-story brick residence. All its windows were dark. There was a front stoop of several steps, and a basement entryway. The windows were all closed, and the place had the look of being unoccupied.

"Not in there, Larry," I answered. "It's closed for the summer—" But I got no further; we heard it again. And this time it sounded, not like a scream, but like a woman's voice calling to attract our attention.

"George! Look there!" Larry cried.

The glow from a street light illumined the basement entryway, and behind one of the dark windows a girl's face was pressed against the pane.

Larry stood gripping me, then drew me forward and down the steps of the entryway. There was a girl in the front basement room. Darkness was behind her, but we could see her white frightened face close to the glass. She tapped on the pane, and in the silence we heard her muffled voice:

"Let me out! Oh, let me get out!"

The basement door had a locked iron gate. I rattled it. "No way of getting in," I said, then stopped short with surprise. "What the devil—"

I joined Larry by the window. The girl was only a few inches from us. She had a pale, frightened face; wide, terrified eyes. Even with that first glimpse, I was transfixed by her beauty. And startled; there was something weird about her. A low-necked, white satin dress disclosed her snowy shoulders; her head was surmounted by a pile of snow-white hair, with dangling white curls framing her pale ethereal beauty. She called again.

"What's the matter with you?" Larry demanded. "Are you alone in there? What is it?"

SHE backed from the window; we could see her only as a white blob in the darkness of the basement room.

I called, "Can you hear us? What is it?"

Then she screamed again. A low scream; but there was infinite terror in it. And again she was at the window.

"You will not hurt me? Let me—oh please let me come out!" Her fists pounded the casement.

What I would have done I don't know. I recall wondering if the policeman would be at our corner down the block; he very seldom was there. I heard Larry saying:

"What the hell!—I'll get her out. George, get me that brick... Now, get back, girl—I'm going to smash the window."

But the girl kept her face pressed against the pane. I had never seen such terrified eyes. Terrified at something behind her in the house; and equally frightened at us.

I call to her: "Come to the door. Can't you come to the door and open it?" I pointed to the basement gate. "Open it! Can you hear me?"

"Yes—I can hear you, and you speak my language. But you—you will not hurt me? Where am I? This—this was my house a moment ago. I was living here."

Demented! It flashed to me. An insane girl, locked in this empty house. I gripped Larry; said to him: "Take it easy; there's something queer about this. We can't smash windows. Let's—"

"You open the door," he called to the girl.

"I cannot."

"Why? Is it locked on the inside?"

"I don't know. Because—oh, hurry! If he—if it comes again—!"

WE could see her turn to look behind her.

Larry demanded, "Are you alone in there?"

"Yes—now. But, oh! a moment ago he was here!"

"Then come to the door."

"I cannot. I don't know where it is. This is so strange and dark a place. And yet it was my home, just a little time ago."

Demented! And it seemed to me that her accent was very queer. A foreigner, perhaps.

She went suddenly into frantic fear. Her fists beat the window glass almost hard enough to shatter it.

"We'd better get her out," I agreed. "Smash it, Larry."

"Yes." He waved at the girl. "Get back. I'll break the glass. Get away so you won't get hurt."

The girl receded into the dimness.

"Watch your hand," I cautioned. Larry took off his coat and wrapped his hand and the brick in it. I gazed behind us. The street was still empty. The slight commotion we had made had attracted no attention.

The girl cried out again as Larry smashed the pane. "Easy," I called to her. "Take it easy. We won't hurt you."

The splintering glass fell inward, and Larry pounded around the casement until it was all clear. The rectangular opening was fairly large. We could see a dim basement room of dilapidated furniture: a door opening into a back room; the girl; nearby, a white shape watching us.

There seemed no one else. "Come on," I said. "You can get out here."

But she backed away. I was half in the window so I swung my legs over the sill. Larry came after me, and together we advanced on the girl, who shrank before us.

Then suddenly she ran to meet us, and I had the sudden feeling that she was not insane. Her fear of us was overshadowed by her terror at something else in this dark, deserted house. The terror communicated itself to Larry and me. Something eery, here.

"Come on," Larry muttered. "Let's get her out of here."

I HAD had indeed no desire to investigate anything further. The girl let us help her through the window. I stood in the entryway holding her arms. Her dress was of billowing white satin with a single red rose at the breast; her snowy arms and shoulders were bare; white hair was piled high on her small head. Her face, still terrified, showed parted red lips; a little round black beauty patch adorned one of her powdered cheeks. The thought flashed to me that this was a girl in a fancy dress costume. This was a white wig she was wearing!

I stood with the girl in the entryway, at a loss what to do. I held her soft warm arms; the perfume of her enveloped me.

"What do you want us to do with you?" I demanded softly. McGuire, the policeman on the block, might at any moment pass. "We might get arrested! What's the matter with you? Can't you explain? Are you hurt?"

She was staring as though I were a ghost, or some strange animal. "Oh, take me away from this place! I will talk— though I do not know what to say—"

Demented or sane, I had no desire to have her fall into the clutches of the police. Nor could we very well take her to our apartment. But there was my friend Dr. Alten, alienist, who lived within a mile of here.

"We'll take her to Alten's," I said to Larry, "and find out what this means. She isn't crazy."

A sudden wild emotion swept me, then. Whatever this mystery, more than anything in the world I did not want the girl to be insane!

Larry said, "There was a taxi down the street.

IT came, now, slowly along the deserted block. The chauffeur had perhaps heard us, and was cruising past to see if we were possible fares. He halted at the curb. The girl had quieted; but when she saw the taxi her face registered wildest terror, and she shrank against me.

"No! No! Don't let it kill me!"

Larry and I were pulling her forward. "What the devil's the matter with you?" Larry demanded again.

She was suddenly wildly fighting with us. "No! That— that mechanism—"

"Get her in it!" Larry panted. "We'll have the neighborhood on us!"

It seemed the only thing to do. We flung her, scrambling and fighting, into the taxi. To the half-frightened, reluctant driver, Larry said vigorously:

"It's all right; we're just taking her to a doctor. Hurry and get us away from here. There's good money in it for you!"

The promise—and the reassurance of the physician's address—convinced the chauffeur. We whirled off toward Washington Square.

Within the swaying taxi I sat holding the trembling girl. She was sobbing now, but quieting.

"There," I murmured. "We won't hurt you; we're just taking you to a doctor. You can explain to him. He's very intelligent."

"Yes," she said softly. "Yes. Thank you. I'm all right now."

She relaxed against me. So beautiful, so dainty a creature.

Larry leaned toward us. "You're better now?"

"Yes."

"That's fine. You'll be all right. Don't think about it."

HE was convinced she was insane. I breathed again the vague hope that it might not be so. She was huddled against me. Her face, upturned to mine, had color in it now; red lips; a faint rose tint in the pale cheeks.

She murmured, "Is this New York?"

My heart sank. "Yes," I answered. "Of course it is."

"But when?"

"What do you mean?"

"I mean, what year?"

"Why, 1935!"

She caught her breath. "And your name is—"

"George Rankin."

"And I..." Her laugh had a queer break in it. "...I am Mistress Mary Atwood. But just a few minutes ago—oh, am I dreaming? Surely I'm not insane!"

Larry again leaned over us. "What are you talking about?"

"You're friendly, you two. Like men; strange, so very strange-looking young men. This—this carriage without any horses—I know now it won't hurt me."

She sat up. "Take me to your doctor. And then to the general of your army. I must see him, and warn him. Warn you all." She was turning half hysterical again. She laughed

11

wildly. "Your general—he won't be General Washington, of course. But I must warn him."

She gripped me. "You think I am demented. But I am not. I am Mary Atwood, daughter of Major Charles Atwood, of General Washington's staff. That was my home, where you broke the window. But it did not look like that a few moments ago. You tell me this is the year 1935, but just a few moments ago I was living in the year 1777!"

CHAPTER TWO
From Out of the Past

"SANE?" said Dr. Alten. "Of course she's sane." He stood gazing down at Mary Atwood. He was a tall, slim fellow, this famous young alienist, with dark hair turning slightly grey at the temples and a neat black mustache that made him look older than he was. Dr. Alten at this time, in spite of his eminence, had not yet turned forty.

"She's sane," he reiterated. "Though from what you tell me, it's a wonder that she is." He smiled gently at the girl. "If you don't mind, my dear, tell us just what happened to you, as calmly as you can."

She sat by an electrolier in Dr. Alten's living room. The yellow light gleamed on her white satin dress, on her white shoulders, her beautiful face with its little round black beauty patch, and the curls of the white wig dangling to her neck. From beneath the billowing, flounced skirt the two satin points of her slippers showed.

A beauty of the year 1777! This thing so strange! I gazed at her with quickened pulse. It seemed that I was dreaming; that as I sat before her in my tweed business suit with its tubular trousers I was the anachronism! This should have been candle-light illumining us; I should have been a powdered and bewigged gallant, in gorgeous satin and frilled shirt to match her dress. How strange, how futuristic we three men of 1935 must have looked to her! And this city through which we had whirled her in the throbbing taxi—no wonder she was overwrought.

Alten fumbled in the pockets of his dressing gown for cigarettes. "Go ahead, Miss Mary. You are among friends. I promise we will try and understand."

SHE smiled. "Yes. I—I believe you." Her voice was low. She sat staring at the floor, choosing her words carefully; and though she stumbled a little, her story was coherent. Upon the wings of her words my fancy conjured that other Time-world, more than a hundred and fifty years ago.

"I was at home to-night," she began. "To-night after dinner. I have no relatives except my father. He is General Washington's aide. We live—our home is north of the city. I was alone, except for the servants.

"Father sent word to-night that he was coming to see me. The messenger got through the British lines. But the redcoats are everywhere. They were quartered in our house. For months I have been little more than a servant to a dozen of My Lord's Howe's officers. They are gentlemen, though: I have no complaint. Then they left, and father, knowing it, wanted to come to see me.

"He should not have tried it. Our house is watched. He promised me he would not wear the British red." She shuddered. "Anything but that—to have him executed as a spy. He would not risk that, but wear merely a long black cloak.

"He was to come about ten o'clock. But at midnight there was no sign of him. The servants were asleep. I sat alone, and every pounding hoof-beat on the road matched my heart.

"Then I went into the garden. There was a dim moon in and out of the clouds. It was hot, like to-night. I mean, why it *was* to-night. It's so strange—"

IN the silence of Alten's living room we could hear the hurried ticking of his little mantle clock, and from the street outside came the roar of a passing elevated train and the honk of a taxi. This was New York of 1935. But to me the crowding ghosts of the past were here. In fancy I saw the white pillars of the moonlit Atwood home. A garden with a dirt road beside it. Red-coated British soldiers passing... And to the south the little city of New York extending northward from crooked Maiden Lane and the Bowling Green...

"Go on, Mistress Mary."

"I sat on a bench in the garden. And suddenly before me there was a white ghost. A shape. A wraith of something which a moment before had not been there. I sat too frightened to move. I could not call out. I tried to, but the sound would not come.

"The shape was like a mist, a little ball of cloud in the center of the garden lawn. Then in a second or two it was solid—a thing like a shining cage, with crisscrossing white bars. It was like a room; a metal cage like a room. I thought that the thing was a phantom or that I was asleep and dreaming. But it was real."

Alten interrupted. "How big was it?"

"As large as this room; perhaps larger. But it was square, and about twice as high as a man."

A cage, then, some twenty feet square and twelve feet high.

She went on: "The cage door opened. I think I was standing, then, and I tried to run but could not. The—the *thing* came from the door of the cage and walked toward me.

It was about ten feet tall. It looked—oh, it looked like a man!"

SHE buried her face in her hands. Again the room was silent. Larry was seated, staring at her; all of us were breathless.

"Like a man?" Alten prompted gently.

"Yes; like a man." She raised her white face. This girl out of the past! Admiration for her swept me anew—she was bravely trying to smile.

"Like a man. A thing with legs, a body, a great round head and swaying arms. A jointed man of metal! You surely must know all about them."

"A Robot!" Larry muttered.

"You have them here, I suppose. Like that rumbling carriage without horses, this jointed iron man came walking toward me. And it spoke! A most horrible hollow voice—but it seemed almost human. And what it said I do not know, for I fainted. I remember falling as it came walking toward me, with stiff-jointed legs.

"When I came to my senses I was in the cage. Everything was humming and glowing. There was a glow outside the bars like a moonlit mist. The iron monster was sitting at a table, with peculiar things—mechanical things—"

"The controls of the cage-mechanisms," said Alten. "How long were you in the cage?"

"I don't know. Time seemed to stop. Everything was silent except the humming noises. They were everywhere. I guess I was only half conscious. The monster sat motionless. In front of him were big round clock faces with whirling hands. Oh, I suppose you don't find this strange; but to me—!"

COULD you see anything outside the cage?" Alten persisted. "No. Just a fog. But it was crawling and shifting. Yes!—I remember now—I could not see anything out there, but I had the thought, the feeling, that there were tremendous things to see! The monster spoke again and told me to be careful; that we were going to stop. Its iron hands pulled at levers. Then the humming grew fainter; died away; and I felt a shock.

"I thought I had fainted again. I could just remember being pulled through the cage door. The monster left me on the ground. It said, 'Lie there, for I will return very soon.'

"The cage vanished. I saw a great cliff of stone near me; it had yellow-lighted openings, high up in the air. And big stone fences hemmed me in. Then I realized I was in an open space between a lot of stone houses. One towered like a cliff, or the side of a pyramid—"

"The back yard of that house on Patton Place!" Larry exclaimed. He looked at me. "Has it any back yard, George?"

"How should I know?" I retorted. "Probably has."

"Go on," Alten was prompting.

"That is nearly all. I found a doorway leading to a dark room. I crawled through it toward a glow of light. I passed through another room. I thought I was in a nightmare, and that this was my home. I remembered that the cage had not moved. It had hardly lurched. Just trembled; vibrated.

"But this was not my home. The rooms were small and dark. Then I peered through a window on a strange stone street. And saw these strange-looking young men. And that is all—all I can tell you."

She had evidently held herself calm by a desperate effort. She broke down now, sobbing without restraint.

CHAPTER THREE
Tugh, the Cripple

THE portals of this mystery had swung wide to receive us. The tumbling events which menaced all our world of 1935 were upon us now. A maelstrom. A torrent in the midst of which we were caught up like tiny bits of cork and whirled away.

But we thought we understood the mystery. We believed we were acting for the best. What we did was no doubt ill-considered; but the human mind is so far from omniscient! And this thing was so strange!

Alten said, "You have a right to be overwrought, Mistress Mary Atwood. But this thing is as strange to us as it is to you. I called that iron monster a Robot. But it does not belong to our age: if it does I have never seen one such as you describe. And traveling through Time—"

He smiled down at her. "That is not a commonplace everyday occurrence to us, I assure you. The difference is that in this world of ours we can understand—or at least explain—these things as being scientific. And so they have not the terror of the supernatural."

Mary was calmer now. She returned his smile. "I realize that; or at least I am trying to realize it."

What a level-headed girl was this! I touched her arm. "You are very wonderful—"

Alten brushed me away. "Let's try and reduce it to rationality. The cage was—is, I should say, since of course it still exists—that cage is a Time-traveling vehicle. It is traveling back and forth through Time, operated by a Robot.

Call it that. A pseudo-human monster fashioned of metal in the guise of a man."

Even Alten had to force himself to speak calmly, as he gazed from one to the other of us. "It came, no doubt from some future age, where half-human mechanisms are common, and Time-traveling is known. That cage probably does not travel in Space, but only in Time. In the future—somewhere—the Space of that house on Patton Place may be the laboratory of a famous scientist. And in the past—in the year 1777—that same Space was the garden of Mistress Atwood's home. So much is obvious. But why—"

"Why," Larry burst out, "did that iron monster stop in 1777 and abduct this girl?"

"And why," I intercepted, "did it stop here in 1935?" I gazed at Mary. "And it told you it would return?"

"Yes."

ALTEN was pondering. "There must be some connection, of course... Mistress Mary, had you never seen this cage before?"

"No."

"Nor anything like it? Was anything like that known to your Time?"

"No. Oh, I cannot truly say that. Some people believe in phantoms, omens and witchcraft. There was in Salem, in the Massachusetts Colony, not so many years ago—"

"I don't mean that. I mean Time-traveling."

"There were soothsayers and fortune-tellers, and necromancers with crystals to gaze into the future."

"We still have them," Alten smiled. "You see, we don't know much more than you do about this thing."

I said, "Did you have any enemy? Anyone who wished you harm?"

She thought a moment. "No—yes, there was one." She shuddered at the memory. "A man—a cripple—a horribly repulsive man of about one score and ten years. He lives down near the Battery." She paused.

"Tell us about him," Larry urged.

She nodded. "But what could he have to do with this? He is horribly deformed. Thin, bent legs, a body like a cask and a bulging forehead with goggling eyes. My Lord Howe's officers say he is very intelligent and very learned. Loyal to the King, too. There was a munitions plot in the Bermudas, and this cripple and Lord Howe were concerned in it. But Father likes the fellow and says that in reality he wishes our cause well. He is rich.

"But you don't want to hear all this. He—he made love to me, and I repulsed him. There was a scene with Father, and Father had our lackeys throw him out. That was a year ago. He cursed horribly. He vowed then that some day he—he would have me; and get revenge on Father. But he has kept away. I have not seen him for a twelvemonth."

WE were silent. I chanced to glance at Alten, and a strange look was on his face.

He said abruptly, "What is this cripple's name, Mistress Mary?"

"Tugh. He is known to all the city as Tugh. Just that. I never heard any Christian name."

Alten rose sharply to his feet. "A cripple named Tugh?"

"Yes," she affirmed wonderingly. "Does it mean anything to you?"

Alten swung on me. "What is the number of that house on Patton Place? Did you happen to notice?"

I had, and wondering I told him.

"Just a minute," he said. "I want to use the phone."

He came back to us in a moment: his face was very solemn. "That house on Patton Place is owned by a man named Tugh! I just called a reporter friend; he remembers a certain case: he confirmed what I thought. Mistress Mary, did this Tugh in your Time ever consult doctors, trying to have his crippled body made whole?"

"Why, of course he did. I have heard that many times. But his crippled, deformed body cannot be cured."

Alten checked Larry and me when we would have broken in with astonished questions. He said:

"Don't ask me what it means; I don't know. But I think that this cripple—this Tugh—has lived both in 1777 and 1935, and is traveling between them in this Time-traveling cage. And perhaps he is the human master of that Robot."

Alten made a vehement gesture. "But we'd better not theorize; it's too fantastic. Here is the story of Tugh in our Time. He came to me some three years ago; in 1932, I think. He offered any price if I could cure his crippled body. All the New York medical fraternity knew him. He seemed sane, but obsessed with the idea that he must have a body like other men. Like Faust, who, as an old man, paid the price of his soul to become youthful, he wanted to have the beautiful body of a young man."

Alten was speaking vehemently. My thoughts ran ahead of his words; I could imagine with grewsome fancy so many things. A cripple, traveling to different ages seeking to be cured. Desiring a different body...

ALTEN was saying, "This fellow Tugh lived alone in that house on Patton Place. He was all you say of him, Mistress Mary. Hideously repulsive. A sinister personality. About thirty years old.

"And, in 1932, he got mixed up with a girl who had a somewhat dubious reputation herself. A dancer, a frequenter of night-clubs, as they used to be called. Her name was Doris Johns—something like that. She evidently thought she could get money out of Tugh. Whatever it was, there was a big uproar. The girl had him arrested, saying that he had assaulted her. The police had quite a time with the cripple."

Larry and I remembered a few of the details of it now, though neither of us had been in New York at the time.

Alten went on: "Tugh fought with the police. Went berserk. I imagine they handled him pretty roughly. In the Magistrate's Court he made another scene, and fought with the court attendants. With ungovernable rage he screamed vituperatives, and was carried kicking, biting and snarling from the court-room. He threatened some wild weird revenge upon all the city officials—even upon the city itself."

"Nice sort of chap," Larry commented.

But Alten did not smile. "The Magistrate could only hold him for contempt of Court. The girl had absolutely no evidence to support her accusation of assault. Tugh was finally dismissed. A week later he murdered the girl.

"The details are unimportant; but he did it. The police had him trapped in his house; had the house surrounded—this same one on Patton Place—but when they burst in to take him, he had inexplicably vanished. He was never heard from again."

Alten continued to regard us with grim, solemn face. "Never heard from—until to-night. And now we hear of him. How he vanished, with the police guarding every exit to that house—well, it's obvious, isn't it? He went into another Time-world. Back to 1777, doubtless."

Mary Atwood gave a little cry. "I had forgotten that I must warn you. Tugh told me once, before Father and I quarreled with him, that he had a mysterious power. He was a most wonderful man, he said. And there was a world in the future—he mentioned 1934 or 1935—which he hated. A great city whose people had wronged him; and he was going to bring death to them. Death to them all! I did not heed him. I thought he was demented, raving…"

ALTEN'S little clock ticked with tumultuous heartbeat through another silence. The great city around us, even though this was two o'clock in the morning, throbbed with a myriad of blended sounds.

A warning! Was the girl from out of the past giving us a warning of coming disaster to this great city?

Alten was pacing the floor. "What are we to do—tell the authorities? Take Mistress Mary Atwood to Police Headquarters and inform them that she has come from the year 1777? And that, if we are not careful, there will be an attack upon New York?"

"No!" I burst out. I could fancy how we would be received at Police Headquarters if we did that! And our pictures in to-morrow's newspapers. Mary's picture, with a jibing headline ridiculing us.

"No," echoed Alten. "I have no intention of doing it. I'm not so foolish as that." He stopped before Mary. "What do you want to do? You're obviously an exceptionally intelligent, level-headed girl. Heaven knows you need to be."

"I—I want to get back home," she stammered.

A pang shot through me as she said it. A hundred and fifty years to separate us. A vast gulf. An impassible barrier.

"That mechanism said it would return!"

"Exactly," agreed Alten. An excitement was upon us all. "Exactly what I mean! Shall we chance it? Try it? There's nothing else I can think of to do. I have a revolver and two hunting rifles."

"Just what do you mean?" I demanded.

"I mean, we'll take my car and go to Tugh's house on Patton Place. Right now! And if that mechanical monster returns, we'll seize it!"

Alten, the usually calm, precise man of science, was tensely vehement. "Seize it! Why not? Three of us, armed, ought to be able to overcome a Robot! Then we'll seize the Time-traveling cage. Perhaps we can operate it. If not, with it in our possession we'll at least have something to show the authorities; there'll be no ridicule then!"

Our inescapable destiny was making us plunge so rashly into this mystery! With the excitement and the strange fantasy of it upon us, we thought we were acting for the best.

Within a quarter of an hour, armed and with a long overcoat and a scarf to hide Mary Atwood's beauty, we took Alten's car and drove to Patton Place.

CHAPTER FOUR
The Fight With the Robot

PATROLMAN McGuire quite evidently had not passed through Patton Place since we left it; or at least he had not noticed the broken window. The house appeared as before, dark, silent, deserted, and the broken basement window yawned with its wide black opening.

"I'll leave the car around on the other street," Alten said as slowly we passed the house. "Quick—no one's in sight; you three get out here."

We crouched in the dim entryway and in a moment he joined us.

I clung to Mary Atwood's arm. "You're not afraid?" I asked.

"No. Yes; of course I am afraid. But I want to do what we planned. I want to go back to my own world, to my Father."

"Inside!" Alten whispered. "I'll go first. You two follow with her."

I can say now that we should not have taken her into that house. It is so easy to look back upon what one might have done!

We climbed through the window, into the dark front basement room. There was only silence, and our faintly padding footsteps on the carpeted floor. The furniture was shrouded with cotton covers standing like ghosts in the gloom. I clutched the loaded rifle which Alten had given me. Larry was similarly armed; and Alten carried a revolver.

"Which way, Mary?" I whispered. "You're sure it was outdoors?"

"Yes. This way, I think."

We passed through the connecting door. The back room seemed to be a dismantled kitchen.

"You stay with her here, a moment," Alten whispered to me. "Come on, Larry. Let's make sure no one—nothing—is down here."

I stood silent with Mary, while they prowled about the lower floor.

"It may have come and gone," I whispered.

"Yes." She was trembling against me.

IT seemed to me an eternity while we stood there listening to the faint footfalls of Larry and Alten. Once they must have stood quiet; then the silence leaped and crowded us. It is horrible to listen to a pregnant silence which every moment might be split by some weird unearthly sound.

Larry and Alten returned. "Seems to be all clear," Alten whispered. "Let's go into the back yard."

The little yard was dim. The big apartment house against its rear wall loomed with a blank brick face, save that there were windows some eight stories up. Only a few windows overlooked this dim area with its high enclosing walls. The space was some forty feet square, and there was a faded grass plot in the center.

We crouched near the kitchen door, with Mary behind us in the room. She said she could recall the cage having stood near the center of the yard, with its door facing this way...

Nearly an hour passed. It seemed that the dawn must be near, but it was only around four o'clock. The same storm clouds hung overhead—a threatening storm which would not break. The heat was oppressing.

"It's come and gone," Larry whispered; "or it isn't coming. I guess that this—"

And then it came! We were just outside the doorway, crouching against the shadowed wall of the house. I had Mary close behind me, my rifle ready.

"There!" whispered Alten.

We all saw it—a faint luminous mist out near the center of the yard—a crawling, shifting ball of fog.

Alten and Larry, one on each side of me, shifted sidewise, away from me. Mary stood and cast off her dark overcoat. We men were in dark clothes, but she stood in gleaming white against the dark rectangle of doorway. It was as we had arranged. A moment only, she stood there; then she moved back, further behind me in the black kitchen.

And in that moment the cage had materialized. We were hoping its occupant had seen the girl, and not us. A breathless moment passed while we stared for the first time at this strange thing from the Unknown... A formless, glowing mist, it quickly gathered itself into solidity. It seemed to shrink. It took form. From a wraith of a cage, in a second it was solid. And so silently, so swiftly, came this thing out of Time into what we call the Present! The dim yard a second ago had been empty.

THE cage stood there, a thing of gleaming silver bars. It seemed to enclose a single room. From within its dim interior came a faint glow, which outlined something standing at the bars, peering out.

The doorway was facing us. There had been utter silence; but suddenly, as though to prove how solid was this apparition, we heard the clank of metal, and the door slid open.

I turned to make sure that Mary was hiding well behind me. The way back to the street, if need for escape arose, was open to her.

I turned again, to face the shining cage. In the doorway something stood peering out, a light behind it. It was a great jointed thing of dark metal some ten feet high. For a moment it stood motionless. I could not see its face clearly, though I knew there was a suggestion of human features, and two great round glowing spots of eyes.

It stepped forward—toward us. A jointed, stiff-legged step. Its arms were dangling loosely; I heard one of its mailed hands clank against its sides.

"Now!" Alten whispered.

I saw Alten's revolver leveling, and my own rifle went up.

"Aim at its face," I murmured.

We pulled our triggers together, and two spurts of flame spat before us. But the thing had stooped an instant before, and we missed. Then came Larry's shot. And then chaos.

I RECALL hearing the ping of Larry's bullet against the mailed body of the Robot. At that it crouched, and from it leaped a dull red-black beam of light. I heard Mary scream. She had not fled but was clinging to me. I cast her off.

"Run! Get back! Get away!" I cried.

Larry shouted, as we all stood bathed in the dull light from the Robot:

"Look out! It sees us!"

He fired again, into the light—and murmured, "Why—why—"

A great surprise and terror was in his tone. Beside me, with half-leveled revolver, Alten stood transfixed. And he too was muttering something.

All this happened in an instant. And there I was aware that I was trying to get my rifle up for firing again; but I could not. My arms stiffened. I tried to take a step, tried to move a foot, but could not. I was rooted there; held, as though by some giant magnet, to the ground!

This horrible dull-red light! It was cold—a frigid, paralyzing blast. The blood ran like cold water in my veins. My feet were heavy with the weight of my body pressing them down.

Then the Robot was moving; coming forward; holding the light upon us. I thought I heard its voice—and a horrible, hollow, rasping laugh.

My brain was chilling. I had confused thoughts; impressions, vague and dreamlike. As though in a dream I felt myself standing there with Mary clinging to me. Both of us were frozen inert upon our feet.

I tried to shout, but my tongue was too thick; my throat seemed swelling inside. I heard Alten's revolver clatter to the stone pavement of the yard. And saw him fall forward—out.

I FELT that in another instant I too would fall. This damnable, chilling light! Then the beam turned partly away, and fell more fully upon Larry. With his youth and greater strength than Alten's or mine, he had resisted its first blast. His weapon had fallen; now he stooped and tried to seize it; but he lost his balance and staggered backward against the house wall.

And then the Robot was upon him. It sprang—this mechanism!—this machine in human form! And, with whatever pseudo-human intelligence actuated its giant metal body, it reached under Larry for his rifle! Its great mailed hand swept the ground, seized the rifle and flung it away. And as Larry twisted sidewise, the Robot's arm with a sweep caught him and rolled him across the yard. When he stopped, he lay motionless.

I heard myself thickly calling to Mary, and the light flashed again upon us. And then we fell forward. Clinging together, we fell...

I did not quite lose consciousness. It seemed that I was frozen, and drifting off half into a nightmare sleep. Great metal arms were gathering Mary and me from the ground. Lifting us; carrying us...

We were in the cage. I felt myself lying on the grid of a metal floor. I could vaguely see the crossed bars of the ceiling overhead, and the latticed walls around me...

THEN the dull-red light was gone. The chill was gone. I was warming. The blessed warm blood again was coursing through my veins, reviving me, bringing back my strength.

I turned over, and found Mary lying beside me. I heard her softly murmur:

"George! George Rankin!"

The giant mechanism clanked the door closed, and came with stiff, stilted steps back into the center of the cage. I heard the hollow rumble of its voice, chuckling, as its hand pulled a switch.

At once the cage-room seemed to reel. It was not a physical movement, though, but more a reeling of my senses, a wild shock to all my being.

Then, after a nameless interval, I steadied. Around me was a humming, glowing intensity of tiny sounds and infinitely small, infinitely rapid vibrations. The whole room grew luminous. The Robot, seated now at a table, showed for a moment as thin as an apparition. All this room—Mary lying beside me, the mechanism, myself—all this was imponderable, intangible, unreal.

And outside the bars stretched a shining mist of movement. Blurred shifting shapes over a vast illimitable vista. Changing things; melting landscapes. Silent, tumbling, crowding events blurred by our movement as we swept past them.

We were traveling through Time!

CHAPTER FIVE
The Girl from 2930

I MUST take up now the sequence of events as Larry saw them. I was separated from Larry during most of the strange incidents which befell us later; but from his subsequent account of what happened to him I am constructing several portions of this history, using my own words based upon Larry's description of the events in which I personally did not participate; I think that this method avoids complications in the narrative and makes more clear my own and Larry's simultaneous actions.

Larry recovered consciousness in the back yard of the house on Patton Place probably only a moment or two after Mary and I had been snatched away in the Time-traveling cage. He found himself bruised and battered, but apparently without injuries. He got to his feet, weak and shaken. His head was roaring.

He recalled what had happened to him, but it seemed like a dream. The back yard was then empty. He remembered vaguely that he had seen the mechanism carry Mary and me into the cage, and that the cage had vanished.

Larry knew that only a few moments had passed. The shots had aroused the neighborhood. As he stood now against the house wall, dizzily looking around, he was aware of calling voices from the nearby windows.

Then Larry stumbled over Alten, who was lying on his face near the kitchen doorway. Still alive, he groaned as Larry fell over him; but he was unconscious.

Forgetting all about his weapon, Larry's first thought was to rush out for help. He staggered through the dark kitchen into the front room, and through the corridor into the street.

Patton Place, as before, was deserted. The houses were dark; the alarm was all in the rear. There were no pedestrians, no vehicles, and no sign of a policeman. Dawn was just coming; as Larry turned eastward he saw, in a patch of clearing sky, stars paling with the coming daylight.

WITH uncertain steps, out in the middle of the street, Larry ran eastward through the middle of the street, hoping that at the next corner he might encounter someone, or find a telephone over which he might call the police.

But he had not gone more than five hundred feet when suddenly he stopped; stood there wavering, panting, staring with whirling senses. Near the middle of the street, with the faint dawn behind it, a ball of gathering mist had appeared directly in his path. It was a luminous, shining mist—and it was gathering into form!

In seconds a small, glowing cage of white luminous bars stood there in the street, where there had just been nothing! It was not the Time-traveling cage from the house yard he had just left. No—he knew it was not that one. This one was similar, but much smaller.

The shock of its appearance held Larry for a moment transfixed. It had so silently, so suddenly appeared in his path that Larry was now within a foot or two of its doorway.

The doorway slid open, and a man leaped out. Behind him, a girl peered from the doorway. Larry stood gaping, wholly confused. The cage had materialized so abruptly that the leaping man collided with him before either man could avoid the other. Larry gripped the man before him; struck out with his fists and shouted. The girl in the doorway called frantically:

"Harl-no noise! Harl-stop him!"

Then, suddenly the two of them were upon Larry and pulling him toward the doorway of the cage. Inside, he was jerked; he shouted wildly; but the girl slammed the door. Then in a soft, girlish voice, in English with a curiously indescribable accent and intonation, the girl said hastily:

"Hold him, Harl! Hold him! I'll start the traveler!"

The black garbed figure of a slim young man was gripping Larry as the girl pulled a switch and there was a shock, a reeling of Larry's senses, as the cage, motionless in Space, sped off into Time...

IT seems needless to encumber this narrative with prolonged details of how Larry explained himself to his two captors. Or how they told him who they were; and from whence they had come; and why. To Larry it was a fantastic—and confusing at first—series of questions and answers. An hour? The words have no meaning. They were traveling through Time. Years were minutes—the words meaning nothing save how they impressed the vehicle's human occupants. To them all it was an interval of mutual distrust which was gradually changing into friendship. Larry found the two strangers singularly direct; singularly forceful in quiet, calm fashion; singularly keen of perception. They had not meant to capture him. The encounter had startled them, and Larry's shouts would have brought others upon the scene.

Almost at once they knew Larry was no enemy, and told him so. And in a moment Larry was pouring out all that had happened to him; and to Alten and Mary Atwood and me. This strange thing! But to Larry now, telling it to these strange new companions, it abruptly seemed not fantastic, but only sinister. The Robot, an enemy, had captured Mary Atwood and me, and whirled us off in the other—the larger—cage.

And in this smaller cage Larry was with friends—for he suddenly found their purpose the same as his! They were chasing this other Time-traveler, with its semi-human, mechanical operator!

The young man said, "You explain to him, Tina. I will watch."

He was a slim, pale fellow, handsome in a queer, tight-lipped, stern-faced fashion. His close-fitting black silk jacket had a white neck ruching and white cuffs; he wore a wide white-silk belt, snug black-silk knee-length trousers and black stockings.

And the girl was similarly dressed. Her black hair was braided and coiled upon her head, and ornaments dangled from her ears. Over her black blouse was a brocaded network jacket; her white belt, compressing her slim waist, dangled with tassels; and there were other tassels on the garters at the knees of her trousers.

She was a pale-faced, beautiful girl, with black brows arching in a thin line, with purple-black eyes like somber pools. She was no more than five feet tall, and slim and frail. But, like her companion, there was about her a queer aspect of calm, quiet power and force of personality—physical vitality merged with an intellect keenly sharp.

She sat with Larry on a little metal bench, listening, almost without interruption, to his explanation. And then, succinctly she gave her own. The young man, Harl, sat at his instruments, with his gaze searching for the other cage, five hundred feet away in Space, but in Time unknown.

And outside the shining bars Larry could vaguely see the blurred, shifting, melting vistas of New York City hastening through the changes Time had brought to it.

THIS young man, Harl, and this girl, Tina, lived in New York City in the Time-world of 2930 A. D. To Larry it was a thousand years in the future. Tina was the Princess of the American Nation. It was an hereditary title, non-political, added several hundred years previously as a picturesque symbol. A tradition; something to make less prosaic the political machine of Republican government. Tina was loved by her people, we afterward came to learn.

Harl was an aristocrat of the New York City of Tina's Time-world, a scientist. In the Government laboratories, under the same roof where Tina dwelt, Harl had worked with another, older scientist, and—so Tina told me—together they had discovered the secret of Time-traveling. They had built two cages, a large and a small, which could travel freely through Time.

The smaller vehicle—this one in which Larry now was speeding—was, in the Time-world of 2930, located in the garden of Tina's palace. The other, somewhat larger, they had built some five hundred feet distant, just beyond the palace walls, within a great Government laboratory.

Harl's fellow scientist—the leader in their endeavors, since he was much older and of wider experience—was not altogether trusted by Tina. He took the credit for the discovery of Time-traveling; yet, said Tina, it was Harl's genius which in reality had worked out the final problems.

And this older scientist was a cripple. A hideously repulsive fellow, named Tugh!

"Tugh!" exclaimed Larry.

"The same," said Tina in her crisp fashion. "Yes—undoubtedly the same. So you see why what you have told us was of such interest. Tugh is a Government leader in our world; and now we find he has lived in *your* Time, and in the Time of this Mary Atwood."

From his seat at the instrument table, Harl burst out: "So he murdered a girl of 1935, and has abducted another of 1777? You would not have me judge him, Tina—"

"No one," she said, "may judge without full facts. This man here—this Larry of 1935—tells us that only a mechanism is in the larger cage—which is what we thought, Harl. And this mechanism, without a doubt, is the treacherous Migul."

THERE was, in 2930, a vast world of machinery. The god of the machine had developed them to almost human intricacy. Almost all the work of the world, particularly in America, and most particularly in the mechanical center of New York City, was done by machinery. And the machinery itself was guided, handled, operated—even, in some instances, constructed—by other, more intricate machines. They were fashioned in pseudo-human form—thinking, logically acting, independently acting mechanisms: the Robots. All but human, they were—a new race. Inferior to humans, yet similar.

And in 2930 the machines, slaves of idle human masters, had been developed too highly! They were upon the verge of a revolt!

All this Tina briefly sketched now to Larry. And to Larry it seemed a very distant, very academic danger. Yet so soon all of us were plunged into the midst of it!

The revolt had not yet come, but it was feared. A great Robot named Migul seemed fomenting it. The revolt was smouldering; at any moment it would burst; and then the machines would rise to destroy the humans.

This was the situation when Harl and Tugh completed the Time-traveling vehicles in this world. They had been tested, but never used. Then Tugh had vanished; was gone now; and the larger of the two vehicles was also gone.

Both Harl and Tina had always distrusted Tugh. They thought him allied to the Robots. But they had no proof; and suavely he denied it, and helped always with the Government activities struggling to keep the mechanical slaves docile and at work.

TUGH and the larger vehicle had vanished, and so had Migul, the insubordinate, giant mechanism—at which, unknown to the Government officials, Tina and Harl had taken the other cage and started in pursuit. It was possible that Tugh was loyal; that Migul had abducted him and stolen the cage.

"Wait!" exclaimed Larry. "I'm trying to figure this out. It seems to hang together. It almost does, but not quite. When did Tugh vanish from your world?"

"To our consciousness," Tina answered, "about three hours ago. Perhaps a little longer than that."

"But look here," Larry protested: "according to my story and that of Mary Atwood, Tugh lived in 1935 and in 1777 for three years."

Confusing? But in a moment Larry understood it. Tugh could have taken the cage, gone to 1777 and to 1935, alternated between them for what was to him, and to those Time-worlds, three years—then have returned to 2930 *on the same day of his departure.* He would have lived these three years; grown that much older; but to the Time-world of 2930 neither he nor the cage would have been missed.

"That," said Tina, "is what doubtless he did. The cage is traveling again. But you, Larry, tell us only Migul is in it."

"I couldn't say that of my own knowledge," said Larry. "Mary Atwood said so. It held only the mechanism you call Migul. And now Migul has with him Mary and my friend George Rankin. We must reach them."

"We want that quite as much as you do," said Harl. "And to find Tugh. If he is a friend we must save him; if a traitor—punish him."

Larry began, "But can you get to the other cage?"

"Only if it stops," said Tina. "*When* it stops, I should say."

"Come here," said Harl. "I will show you."

LARRY crossed the glowing room. He had forgotten its aspect—the ghostly unreality around him. He too—his body, like Harl's and Tina's—was of the same wraith-like substance... Then, suddenly, Larry's viewpoint shifted. The room and its occupants were real and tangible. And outside the glowing bars—everything out there was the unreality.

"Here," said Harl. "I will show you. It is not visible yet."

Each of the cages was equipped with an intricate device, strange of name, which Larry and I have since termed a Time-telespectroscope. Larry saw it now as a small metal box, with tuning vibration dials, batteries, coils, a series of tiny prisms and an image-mirror—the whole surmounted by what appeared the barrel of a small telescope. Harl had it leveled and was gazing through it.[1] *(for footnotes see pg. 188)*

The enemy cage was not visible, now. But Harl and Tina had glimpsed it on several occasions. What vast realms Time opens within a single small segment of Space! The larger vehicle seemed speeding back and forth. A dash into the year 1777! as Larry learned from Mary Atwood.

And there had been several evidences of the cage halting in 1935. Larry's account explained two such pauses. But the others? Those others, which brought to the City of New York such amazing disaster? We did not learn of then until much later. But Alten lived through them, and presently I shall reconstruct them from his account.

The larger cage was difficult to trace in its sweep along the corridors of Time. Never once had Tina and Harl been able to stop simultaneously with it, for a year has so many separate days and hours. The nearest they came was the halt in the night of June 8-9, when they encountered Larry, and, startled, seized him and moved on again.

HARL continued to gaze through the eyepiece of the detecting instrument. But nothing showed, and the mirror-grid on the table was dark.

"But—which way are we going?" Larry stammered.

"Back," said Tina. "The retrograde... Wait! Do not do that!"

Larry had turned toward where the bars, less luminous, showed a dark rectangle like a window. The desire swept him to gaze out at the shining, changing scene.

But Tina checked him. "Do not do that! Not yet! It is too great a shock in the retrograde. It was to me."

"But where are we?"

In answer she gestured toward a series of tiny dials on the table edge. There were at least two score of them, laid in a triple bank. Dials to record the passing minutes, hours, days; the years, the centuries! Larry stared at the small whirring pointers. Some were a blur of swift whirling movement—the hours and days. Tina showed Larry how to read them. The cage was passing through the year 1880. In a few moments of Larry's consciousness it was 1799. Then 1793. The infant American nation was here now. But with the cage retrograding, soon they would be in the Revolutionary War.

Tina said. "The other cage may go back to 1777, if Tugh meant ill to Mary Atwood, or wants revenge upon her father, at you said. We shall see."

They had reached 1790 when Harl gave a low ejaculation.

"You see it?" Tina murmured.

"Yes. Very faintly."

Larry bent tensely forward. "Will it show on the mirror?"

"Yes; presently. We are about ten years from it. If we get closer, the mirror will show it."

But the mirror held dark. No—now it was glowing a trifle. A vague luminosity.

Tina moved toward the instrument controls nearby. "Watch closely, Harl. I will slow us down."

IT seemed to Larry that the humming with which everything around him was endowed, now began descending in pitch. And his head suddenly was unsteady. A singular, wild, queer feeling was within him. An unrest. A tugging torment of every tiny cell of his body.

Tina said. "Hold steady, Larry, for when we stop."

"Will it shock me?"

"Yes—at first. But the shock will not harm you: it is nearly all mental."

The mirror held an image now—the other cage. Larry saw, on the six-inch square mirror surface, a crawling, melting scene of movement. And in the midst of it, the image of the other cage, faint and spectral. In all the mirrored movement, only the apparition of the cage was still. And this marked it; made it visible.

Over an interval, while Larry stared, the ghostly image grew plainer. They were approaching its Time-factor!

"It is stopping," Harl murmured. Larry was aware that he had left the eyepiece and joined Tina at the controls.

"Tina, let us try to get it right this time."

"Yes."

"In 1777; but which month, would you say?"

"It has stopped! See?"

LARRY heard them clicking switches, and setting the controls for a stop. Then he felt Tina gently push him.

"Sit here. Standing, you might fall."

He found himself on a bench. He could still see the mirror. The ghost of the other cage was now lined more plainly upon it.

"This month," said Tina, setting a switch. "Would not you say so? And this day."

"But the hour, Tina? The minute?"

The vast intricate corridors of Time!

"It would be in the night. Hasten, Harl, or we will pass! Try the night—around midnight. Even Migul has the mechanical intelligence to fear a daylight pausing."

The controls were set for the stop. Larry heard Tina murmuring, "Oh, I pray we may have judged with correctness!"

The vehicle was rapidly coming to a stop. Larry gripped the table, struggling to hold firm to his reeling senses. This soundless, grinding halt! His swaying gaze strayed from the mirror. Outside the glowing bars he could now discern the luminous greyness separating. Swift, soundless claps of light and dark, alternating. Daylight and darkness. They had been blended, but now they were separating. The passing, retrograding days—a dozen to the second of Larry's consciousness. Then fewer. Vivid daylight. Black night. Daylight again.

"Not too slowly, Harl; we will be seen...! Oh, it is gone!"

Larry saw the mirror go blank. The image on it had flared to great distinctness, faded, and was gone. Darkness was around Larry. Then daylight. Then darkness again.

"Gone!" echoed Harl's disappointed voice. "But it stopped here…! Shall we stop, Tina?"

"Yes! Leave the control settings as they are. Larry—be careful, now."

A dragging second of grey daylight. A plunge into night. It seemed to Larry that all the universe was soundlessly reeling. Out of the chaos, Tina was saying:

"We have stopped. Are you all right, Larry?"

"Yes," he stammered.

HE stood up. The cage room, with its faint lights, benches and settles, instrument tables and banks of controls, was flooded with moonlight from outside the bars. Night, and the moon and stars out there.

Harl slid the door open. "Come, let us look."

The reeling chaos had fallen swiftly from Larry. With Tina's small black and white figure beside him, he stood at the threshold of the cage. A warm gentle night breeze fanned his face.

A moonlit landscape lay somnolent around the cage. Trees were nearby. The cage stood in a corner of a field by a low picket fence. Behind the trees, a ribbon of road stretched away toward a distant shining river. Down the road some five hundred feet, the white columns of a large square brick house gleamed in the moonlight. And behind the house was a garden and a group of barns and stables.

The three in the cage doorway stood whispering, planning. Then two of them stepped to the ground. They were Larry and Tina; Harl remained to guard the cage.

The two figures on the ground paused a moment and then moved cautiously along the inside line of the fence toward the home of Major Atwood. Strange anachronisms, these two prowling figures! A girl from the year 2930; a man from 1935!

And this was revolutionary New York, now. The little city lay well to the south. It was open country up here. The New York of 1935 had melted away and was gone...

This was a night in August of 1777.

CHAPTER SIX
The New York Massacre of 1935

DR. ALTEN recovered consciousness in the back yard of the house on Patton Place just a few moments after Larry had encountered the smaller Time-traveling cage and been carried off by Harl and Tina. Previously to that, of course, the mysterious mechanism in the guise of a giant man had abducted Mary Atwood and me in the larger Time-cage.

Alten became aware that people were bending over him. The shots we had taken at the Robot had aroused the neighborhood. A policeman arrived.

The sleeping neighbors had heard the shots, but it seemed that none had seen the cage, or the metal man who had come from it. Alten said nothing. He was taken to the nearest police station where grudgingly, he told his story. He was laughed at; reprimanded for alcoholism. Evidently, according to the police sergeant, there had been a fight, and Alten had drawn the loser's end. The police confiscated the two rifles and the revolver and decided that no one but Alten had been hurt. But at best it was a queer affair. Alten had not been shot; he was just stiff with cold; he said a dull-red ray had fallen upon him and stiffened him with its frigid blast. Utter nonsense!

Dr. Alten was a man of standing. It was a reprehensible affair, but he was released upon his own recognizance. He was charged with breaking into the untenanted home of one Tugh; of illegally possessing firearms; of disturbing the peace—a variety of offenses all rational to the year 1935.

BUT Alten's case never reached even its hearing in the Magistrate's Court. He arrived home just after dawn, that June 9, still cold and stiff from the effects of the ray, and bruised and battered by the sweeping blow of Miguel's great iron arm. He recalled vaguely seeing Larry fall, and the iron monster bearing Mary Atwood and me away. What had happened to Larry, Alten could not guess, unless the Robot had returned, ignored him and taken his friend away.

During that day of June 9 Alten summoned several of his scientific friends, and to them he told fully what had happened to him. They listened with a keen understanding and a rational knowledge of the possibility that what he said was true; but credibility they could not give him.

The noon papers came out.

NOTED ALIENIST ATTACKED BY GHOST Felled by One of the Fantastic Monsters of His Brain

A jocular, jibing account. Then Alten gave it up. He had about decided to plead guilty in the Magistrate's Court to disorderly conduct and all the rest of it! That was preferable to being judged a liar, or insane.

AND then, at about 9 P.M. on the evening of June 9, the first of the mechanical monsters came stalking from the house on Patton Place—the beginning of the revenge which Tugh had threatened when arrested. The policeman at the corner—one McGuire—turned in the first hysterical alarm. He rushed into a little candy and stationery store shouting that he had seen a piece of machinery running wild. His telephone call brought a squad of his comrades. The Robot at first did no damage.

McGuire later told how he saw it as it emerged from the entryway of the Tugh house. It came lurching out into the street—a giant thing of dull grey metal, with tubular, jointed legs; a body with a great bulging chest; a round head, eight or ten feet above the pavement; eyes that shot fire.

The policeman took to his heels. There was a commotion in Patton Place during those next few minutes. Pedestrians saw the thing standing in the middle of the street, staring stupidly around it. The head wobbled. Some said that the eyes shot fire; others, that it was not the eyes, but more like a torch in its mailed hand. The torch shot a small beam of light around the street—a beam which was dull-red.

The pedestrians fled. Their cries brought people to the nearby house windows. Women screamed. Presently bottles were thrown from the windows. One of these crashed against the iron shoulder of the monster. It turned its head: as though its neck were rubber, some said. And it gazed upward, with a human gesture as though it were not angry, but contemptuous.

But still, beyond a step or two in one direction or another, it merely stood and waved its torch. The little dull-red beam of light carried no more than twenty or thirty feet. The street in a few moments was clear of pedestrians; remained littered with glass from the broken bottles. A taxi came suddenly around the corner, and the driver, with an almost immediate tire puncture, saw the monster. He hauled up to the curb, left his cab and ran.

THE Robot saw the taxicab, and stood gazing. It turned its torch-beam on it, and seemed surprised that the thing did not move. Then thinking evidently that this was a less cowardly enemy than the humans, it made a rush to it. The chauffeur had not turned off his engine when he fled, so the cab stood throbbing.

The Robot reached it; cuffed it with a huge mailed fist. The windshield broke; the windows were shattered; but the cab stood purring, planted upon its four wheels.

Strange encounter! They say that the Robot tried to talk to it. At last, exasperated, it stepped backward, gathered itself and pounced on it again. Stooping, it put one of its great arms down under the wheels, the other over the hood, and with prodigious strength heaved the cab into the air. It crashed on its side across the street, and in a moment was covered with flames.

It was about this time that Patrolman McGuire came back to the scene. He shot at the monster a few times; hit it, he was sure. But the Robot did not heed him.

The block was now in chaos. People stood at most of the windows, crowds gathered at the distant street corners, while the blazing taxicab lighted the block with a lurid glare. No one dared approach within a hundred feet or so of the monster. But when, after a time, it showed no disposition to attack, throngs at every distinct point of vantage tried to gather where they could see it. Those nearest reported back that its face was iron; that it had a nose, a wide, yawning mouth, and holes for eyes. There were certainly little lights in the eye-holes.

A small, fluffy white dog went dashing up to the monster and barked bravely at its heels. It leaped nimbly away when the Robot stooped to seize it. Then, from the Robot's chest, the dull-red torch beam leaped out and down. It caught the little dog, and clung to it for an instant. The dog stood transfixed; its bark turned to a yelp; then a gurgle. In a moment it fell on its side; then lay motionless with stiffened legs sticking out.

ALL this happened within five minutes. McGuire's riot squad arrived, discreetly ranged itself at the end of the block and fired. The Robot by then had retreated to the entryway of the Tugh house, where it stood peering as though with curiosity at all this commotion. There came a clanging from the distance: someone had turned in a fire alarm. Through the gathered crowds and vehicles the engines came tearing up.

Presently there was not one Robot, but three: a dozen! More than that, many reports said. But certain it is that within half an hour of the first alarm, the block in front of Tugh's home held many of the iron monsters. And there were many human bodies lying strewn there, by then. A few policemen had made a stand at the corner, to protect the crowd against one of the Robots. The thing had made an unexpected infuriated rush...

There was a panic in the next block, when a thousand people suddenly tried to run. A score of people were trampled under foot. Two or three of the Robots ran into that next block—ran impervious to the many shots which now were fired at them. From what was described as slots in the sides of their iron bodies they drew swords—long, dark, burnished blades. They ran, and at each fallen human body they made a single stroke of decapitation, or, more generally, cut the body in half.

The Robots did not attack the fire engines. Emboldened by this, firemen connected a hose and pumped a huge jet of water toward the Tugh house. The Robots then rushed it. One huge mechanism—some said it was twelve feet tall—ran heedlessly into the firemen's high-pressure stream, toppled backward from the force of the water and very strangely lay still. Killed? Rather, out of order: deranged: it was not human, to be killed. But it lay motionless, with the fire hose playing upon it. Then abruptly there was an explosion. The fallen Robot, with a deafening report and a puff of green flame, burst into flying metallic fragments like shrapnel. Nearby windows were broken from the violent explosion, and pieces of the flying metal were hurled a hundred feet or more. One huge chunk, evidently a plate of the thing's body, struck into the crowd two blocks away, and felled several people.

At this smashing of one of the mechanisms, its brother Robots went for the first time into aggressive action. A hundred or more were pouring now from the vacant house of the absent Tugh...

THE alarm by ten o'clock had spread throughout the entire city. Police reserves were called out, and by midnight soldiers were being mobilized. Panics were starting everywhere. Millions of people crowded in on small Manhattan Island, in the heart of which was this strange enemy.

Panics... Yet human nature is very strange. Thousands of people started to leave Manhattan, but there were other thousands during that first skirmish who did their best to try and get to the neighborhood of Patton Place to see what was going on. They added greatly to the confusion. Traffic soon was stalled everywhere. Traffic officers, confused, frightened by the news which was bubbled at them from every side, gave wrong orders; accidents began to occur. And then, out of the growing confusion, came tangles, until, like a dammed stream, all the city mid-section was paralyzed. Vehicles were abandoned everywhere.

Reports of what was happening on Patton Place grew more confused. The gathering nearby crowds impeded the police and firemen. The Robots, by ten o'clock, were using a single great beam of dull-red light. It was two or three feet broad. It came from a spluttering, hissing cylinder mounted on runners which the Robots dragged along the ground, and the beam was like that of a great red searchlight. It swung the length of Patton Place in both directions. It hissed against the houses; penetrated the open windows which now were all deserted; swept the front cornices of the roofs, where crowds of tenants and others were trying to hide. The red beam drove back the ones near the edge, except those who were stricken by its frigid blast and dropped like plummets into the street, where the Robots with flashing blades pounced upon them.

Frigid was the blast of this giant light-beam. The street, wet from the fire-hose, was soon frozen with ice—ice which increased under the blast of the beam, and melted in the warm air of the night when the ray turned away.

From every distant point in the city, awed crowds could see that great shaft when it occasionally shot upward, to stain the sky with blood.

DR. ALTEN by midnight was with the city officials, telling them what he could of the origin of this calamity. They were a distracted group indeed! There were a thousand things to do, and frantically they were giving orders, struggling to cope with conditions so suddenly unprecedented. A great city, millions of people, plunged into conditions unfathomable. And every moment growing worse. One calamity bringing another, in the city, with its myriad diverse activities so interwoven. Around Alten the clattering, terrifying reports were surging. He sat there nearly all that night; and near dawn, an official plane carried him in a flight over the city.

The panics, by midnight, were causing the most deaths. Thousands, hundreds of thousands, were trying to leave the island. The tube trains, the subways, the elevateds were jammed. There were riots without number in them. Ferryboats and bridges were thronged to their capacity. Downtown Manhattan, fortunately comparatively empty, gave space to the crowds plunging down from the crowded foreign quarters bordering Greenwich Village. By dawn it was estimated that five thousand people had been trampled to death by the panics in various parts of the city, in the tubes beneath the rivers and on departing trains.

And another thousand or more had been killed by the Robots. How many of these monstrous metal men were now in evidence, no one could guess. A hundred—or a thousand. The Time-cage made many trips between that night of June 9 and 10, 1935, and a night in 2930. Always it gauged its return to this same night.

The Robots poured out into Patton Place. With running, stiff-legged steps, flashing swords, small light-beams darting before them, they spread about the city...

CHAPTER SEVEN
The Vengeance of Tugh

A MYRIAD individual scenes of horror were enacted. Metal travesties of the human form ran along the city streets, overturning stalled vehicles, climbing into houses, roaming dark hallways, breaking into rooms.

There was a woman who afterward told that she crouched in a corner, clutching her child, when the door of her room was burst in. Her husband, who had kept them there thinking it was the safest thing to do, fought futilely with the great thing of iron. Its sword slashed his head from his body with a single stroke. The woman and the little child screamed, but the monster ignored them. They had a radio, tuned to a station in New Jersey which was broadcasting the events. The Robot seized the instrument as though in a frenzy of anger, tore it apart, then rushed from the room.

No one could give a connected picture of the events of that horrible night. It was a series of disjointed incidents out of which the imagination must construct the whole.

The panics were everywhere. The streets were stalled with traffic and running, shouting, fighting people. And the area around Greenwich Village brought reports of continued horror.

The Robots were of many different forms; some pseudo-human; others, great machines running amuck—things more monstrous, more horrible even, than those which mocked humanity. There was a great pot-bellied monster which forced its way somehow to a roof. It encountered a crouching woman and child in a corner of the parapet, seized them, one in each of its great iron hands, and whirled them out over the housetops.

BY dawn it seemed that the Robots had mounted several projectors of the giant red beam on the roofs of Patton Place. They held a full square mile, now, around Tugh's house. The police and firemen had long since given up fighting them. They were needed elsewhere—the police to try and cope with the panics, and the firemen to fight the conflagrations which everywhere began springing up. Fires, the natural outcome of chaos; and fires, incendiary—made by criminals who took advantage of the disaster to fatten like ghouls upon the dead. They prowled the streets. They robbed and murdered at will.

The giant beams of the Robots carried a frigid blast for miles. By dawn of that June 10th, the south wind was carrying from the enemy area a perceptible wave of cold even as far as Westchester. Allen, flying over the city, saw the devastated area clearly. Ice in the streets—smashed vehicles—the gruesome litter of sword-slashed human bodies. And other human bodies, plucked apart; strewn...

Alten's plane flew at an altitude of some two thousand feet. In the growing daylight the dark prowling figures of the metal men were plainly seen. There were no humans left alive in the captured area. The plane dropped a bomb into Washington Square where a dozen or two of the Robots were gathered. It missed them. The plane's pilot had not realized that they were grouped around a projector; its red shaft sprang up, caught the plane and clung to it. Frigid blast! Even at that two thousand feet altitude, for a few seconds Alten and the others were stiffened by the cold. The motor missed; very nearly stopped. Then an intervening rooftop cut off the beam, and the plane escaped.

ALL this I have pictured from what Dr. Alten subsequently told me. He leaves my narrative now, since fate hereafter held him in the New York City of 1935. But he has described for me three horrible days, and three still more horrible nights. The whole world now was alarmed. Every nation offered its forces of air and land and sea to overcome these gruesome invaders. Warships steamed for New York harbor. Soldiers were entrained and brought to the city outskirts. Airplanes flew overhead. On Long Island, Staten Island, and in New Jersey, infantry, tanks and artillery were massed in readiness.

But they were all very nearly powerless to attack. Manhattan Island still was thronged with refugees. It was not possible for the millions to escape; and for the first day there were hundreds of thousands hiding in their homes. The city could not be shelled. The influx of troops was hampered by the outrush of civilians.

By the night of the tenth, nevertheless, ten thousand soldiers were surrounding the enemy area. It embraced now all the mid-section of the island. The soldiers rushed in. Machine-guns were set up.

But the Robots were difficult to find. With this direct attack they began fighting with an almost human caution. Their bodies were impervious to bullets, save perhaps in the orifices of the face which might or might not be vulnerable. But when attacked, they skulked in the houses, or crouched like cautious animals under the smashed vehicles. Then there were times when they would wade forward directly into machine-gun fire—unharmed—plunging on until the gunners fled and the Robots wreaked their fury upon the abandoned gun.

The only hand-to-hand conflicts took place on the afternoon of June 10th. A full thousand soldiers were killed—and possibly six or eight of the Robots. The troops were ordered away after that; they made lines across the island to the north and to the south, to keep the enemy from increasing its area. Over Greenwich Village now, the circling planes—at their highest altitude, to avoid the upflung crimson beams—dropped bombs. Hundreds of houses there were wrecked. Tugh's house could not be positively identified, though the attack was directed at it most particularly. Afterward, it was found by chance to have escaped.

THE night of June 10th brought new horrors. The city lights failed. Against all the efforts of the troops and the artillery fire which now was shelling the Washington Square area, the giant mechanisms pushed north and south. By midnight, with their dull-red beams illumining the darkness of the canyon streets, they had reached the Battery, and spread northward beyond the northern limits of Central Park.

It is estimated that by then there were still a million people on Manhattan Island.

The night of the 11th, the Robots made their real attack. Those who saw it, from planes overhead, say that upon a roof near Washington Square a machine was mounted from which a red beam sprang. It was not of parallel rays, like the others; this one spread. And of such power it was, that it painted the leaden clouds of the threatening, overcast night. Every plane, at whatever high altitude, felt its frigid blast and winged hastily away to safety.

Spreading, dull-red beam! It flashed with a range of miles. Its light seemed to cling to the clouds, staining like blood; and to cling to the air itself with a dull lurid radiance.

It was a hot night, that June 11th, with a brewing thunderstorm. There had been occasional rumbles of thunder and lightning flashes. The temperature was perhaps 90° F.

Then the temperature began falling. A million people were hiding in the great apartment houses and homes of the northern sections, or still struggling to escape over the littered bridges or by the paralyzed transportation systems—and that million people saw the crimson radiance and felt the falling temperature.

80°. Then 70°. Within half an hour it was at 30°! In unheated houses, in midsummer, in the midst of panic, the people were swept by chilling cold. With no adequate clothing available they suffered greatly—and then abruptly they were freezing. Children wailing with the cold; then asleep in numbed, last slumber...

Zero weather in midsummer! And below zero! How cold it got, there is no one to say. The abandoned recording instrument in the Weather Bureau was found, at 2:16 A.M., the morning of June 12, 1935, to have touched minus 42° F.

The gathering storm over the city burst with lightning and thunder claps through the blood-red radiance. And then snow began falling. A steady white downpour, a winter blizzard with the lightning flashing above it, and the thunder crashing.

With the lightning and thunder and snow, crazy winds sprang up. They whirled and tossed the thick white snowflakes; swept in blasts along the city streets. It piled the snow in great drifts against the houses; whirled and sucked it upward in white powdery geysers.

AT 2:30 A.M. there came a change. The dull-red radiance which swept the city changed in color. Through the shades of the spectrum it swung up to violet. And no longer was it a blast of cold, but of heat! Of what inherent temperature the ray of that spreading beam may have been, no one can say. It caught the houses, and everything inflammable burst into flame. Conflagrations were everywhere—a thousand spots of yellow-red flames, like torches, with smoke rolling up from them to mingle with the violet glow overhead.

The blizzard was gone. The snow ceased. The storm clouds rolled away, blasted by the pendulum winds which lashed the city.

By 3 A.M. the city temperature was over 100° F—the dry, blistering heat of a midsummer desert. The northern city streets were littered with the bodies of people who had rushed from their homes and fallen in the heat, the wild winds and the suffocating smoke outside.

And then, flung back by the abnormal winds, the storm clouds crashed together overhead. A terrible storm, born of outraged nature, vent itself on the city. The fires of the burning metropolis presently died under the torrent of falling water. Clouds of steam whirled and tossed and hissed close overhead, and there was a boiling hot rain.

By dawn the radiance of that strange spreading beam died away. The daylight showed a wrecked, dead city. Few humans indeed were left alive on Manhattan that dawn. The Robots and their apparatus had gone...

The vengeance of Tugh against the New York City of 1935 was accomplished.

Where nothing had been stood a cage

CHAPTER EIGHT
The Murder of Major Atwood

WE are late," Tina whispered. It was that night in 1777 when she, Larry and Harl stepped from their Time-traveling cage; and again I am picturing the events as Larry afterward described them to me. "Migul, in the other cage, was here," Tina added. "But it's gone now. Exactly where was it, I wonder?"

"Mary Atwood said it appeared in the garden."

They crept down the length of the field, just inside the picket fence. In a moment the trees and an intervening hillock of ground hid the dimly shining outline of their own cage from their sight. The dirt road leading to Major Atwood's home was on the other side of the fence.

"Wait," murmured Tina. "There is a light in the house. Someone is awake."

"When was Migul here, do you think?" Larry whispered.

"Last night, perhaps. Or to-night. It may be only an hour—or a few minutes ago."

The faint thud of horses' hoofs on the roadway made Tina and Larry drop to the ground. They crouched in the shadows of a tree. Galloping horses were approaching along the road. The moon went under a cloud.

From around a bend in the road a group of horsemen came. They were galloping; then they slowed to a trot; a walk. They reined up in the road not more than twenty feet from Larry and Tina. In the starlight they showed clearly— men in the red and white uniform of the army of the King. Some of them wore short, dark cloaks. They dismounted with a clanking of swords and spurs.

THEIR voices were audible. "Leave the steeds with Jake. Egad, we've made enough noise already."

"Here, Jake, you scoundrel. Stay safely here with the mounts."

"Come on, Tony. You and I will circle. We have him, this time. By the King's garter, what a fool he is to come into New York at such a time!"

"He wants to see his daughter, I venture."

"Right, Tony. And have you seen her? As saucy a little minx as there it in the Colonies. I was quartered here last month. I do not blame the major for wanting to come."

"Here, take my bridle, Jake. Tie them to the fence."

There was a swift confusion of voices; laughter. "If you should hear a pistol shot, Jake, ride quickly back and tell My Lord there was a fracas and you did not dare remain."

"I only hope he is garbed in the rebel white and blue—eh, Tony? Then he will yield like an officer and a gentleman; which he is, rebel or no."

They were moving away to surround the house. Two were left.

"Come on, Tony. We will pound the front knocker in the name of the King. A feather in our cap when we ride him down to the Bowling Green and present him to My Lord..."

The voices faded.

Larry gripped the girl beside him. "They are British soldiers going to capture Major Atwood! What can we—"

HE never finished. A scream echoed over the somnolent night—a voice from the rear of the house. A man's voice.

The red-coated soldiers ran forward. In the field, close against the fence, Tina and Larry were running.

From the garden of the house a man was screaming. Then there were other voices; servants were awakening in the upper rooms. The screaming, shouting man rushed through the house. He appeared at the front door, standing between the high white colonial pillars which supported the overhead porch. A yellow light fell upon him through the opened doorway. An old, white-headed negro appeared. Larry and Tina, in the nearby field, stood stricken by the scene.

"The marster—the marster—" He shouted this wildly.

The British officers ran at him.

"You, Thomas, tell us where the major is. We've come for him; we know he's here! Don't lie!"

"But the marster—" He choked over it.

"A trick, Tony! Egad, if he is trying to trick us—"

They leaped to the porch and seized the old negro.

"Speak, you devil!" They shook him. "The house is surrounded. He cannot escape!"

"But the marster is—is dead! My girl Tollie saw it and then she swooned." He steadied himself. "He—the major's in the garden, Marster Tony. Lying there dead! Murdered!

By a ghost, Tollie says. A great, white, shining ghost that came to the garden and murdered him!"

IF you were to delve very closely into certain old records of Revolutionary New York City during the year 1777, you doubtless would find mention of the strange murder of Major Atwood, who, coming from New Jersey, is thought to have crossed the river well to the north of the city, mounted his horse—which, by pre-arrangement, one of his retainers had left for him somewhere to the south of Dykeman's farm— and ridden to his home. He came, not as a spy, but in full uniform. And no sooner had he reached his home when he was strangely murdered. There was only a negro tale of an apparition which had appeared in the garden and murdered the master.

Larry and I have found cursory mention of that. But I doubt if the group of My Lord Howe's gay young blades who were sent north to capture Major Atwood ever reported exactly what happened to them. The old Dutch ferryman divulged that he had been hired to ferry the homecoming major; this, too, is recorded. But Tony Green and his fellow officers, sent to apprehend the colonial major, found him inexplicably murdered; and by dawn they were back at the Bowling Green, white-faced and shaken.

They told some of what had happened to them, but not all. They could not expect to be believed, for instance, if they said that though they were unafraid of a negro's tale of a ghost, they had themselves encountered two ghosts, and had fled the premises!

Those two ghosts were only Larry and Tina!

The negro babbled of a shining cage appearing in the garden. That, of course, was undoubtedly set down as nonsense. Tony Green and his friends went to the garden and examined the body of Major Atwood. What had killed him no one could say. No bullet had struck him. There were no wounds, no knife thrust, no sword slash. Tony held the lantern with its swaying yellow glow close to the murdered man's body. The August night was warm; the garden, banked by trees and shrubbery, was breathless and oppressively hot; yet the body of Atwood seemed frozen! He had been dead but a short while, and already the body was stiff. More than that, it was ice cold. The face, the brows were wet as though frost had been there and now was melted!

Tony Green's hand shook as he held the lantern. He tried to tell his comrades that Atwood had died from failure of the heart. Undoubtedly it was that. He had seen what he supposed was an apparition; something had frightened him; and a weak heart had brought his death.

THEN, in another part of the garden, one of the searching officers found a sheet of parchment scroll with writing on it. Yet it was not parchment, either. Some strange, white, smooth fabric which crumpled and tore very easily, the like of which this young British officer of Howe's staff had never seen before. It was found lying in a flower bed forty or fifty feet from Atwood's body. They gathered in a group to examine it by the light of the lantern. Writing! The delicate script of Mary Atwood! A missive addressed to her father. It was strangely written, evidently not with a quill.

Tony read it with an awed, frightened voice:

"Father, beware of Tugh! Beware of Tugh! And, my dear Father, good-by. I am departing, I think, to the year of our Lord, 2930. Cannot explain—a captive—good-by—nothing you can do—

Mary."

Strange! I can imagine how strange they thought it was. Tugh—why he was the cripple who had lived down by the Bowling Green, and had lately vanished!

They were reading this singularly unexplainable missive, when as though to climax their own fears of the supernatural they saw themselves a ghost! And not only one ghost, but two!

Plain as a pikestaff, peering from a nearby tree, in a shaft of moonlight, a ghost was standing. It was the figure of a young girl, with jacket and breeches of black and gleaming white. An apparition fantastic! And a young man was with her, in a long dark jacket and dark tubular pipes, for legs.

THE two ghosts with dead white faces stood peering. Then the man moved forward. His dead, strange voice called:

"Drop that paper!"

My Lord Howe's red-coated officers dropped the parchment and fled.

And later, when Atwood's body was taken away to be given burial as befitted an enemy officer and a gentleman, that missive from Mary Atwood had disappeared. It was never found.

Tony Green and his fellows said nothing of this latter incident. One cannot with grace explain being routed by a ghost. Not an officer of His Majesty's army!

Unrecorded history! A supernatural incident of the year 1777!

Undoubtedly in the past ages there have been many such affairs: some never recorded, others interwoven in written history and called supernatural.

Yet why must they be that? There was nothing supernatural in the events of that night in Major Atwood's garden.

Is this perchance an explanation of why the pages of history are so thronged with tales of ghosts? There must, indeed, be many future ages down the corridors of Time where the genius of man will invent devices to fling him back into his past. And the impressions upon the past which he makes are called supernatural.

Whether this be so or not, it was so in the case of these two Time-traveling vehicles from 2930. Larry and I think that the world of 1935 is just now shaking off the shackles of superstition, and coming to realize that what is called the supernatural is only the Unknown. Who can say, up to 1935, how many Time-traveling humans have come briefly back? Is this, perchance, what we call the phenomena of the supernatural?

LARRY and Tina—anything but ghosts, very much alive and very much perturbed—were standing back of that tree. They saw the British officers reading the scrap of paper. They could hear only the words, "Mary," and "from Mistress Atwood."

"A message!" Larry whispered. "She and George must have found a chance to write it, and dropped it here while the Robot murdered Major Atwood!"

Larry and Tina vehemently wanted to read the note. Tina whispered:

"If we show ourselves, they will be frightened and run. It is nearly always so where Harl and I have become visible in earlier Times."

"Yes. I'll try it."

Larry stepped from the tree, and shouted, "Drop that paper!"

And a moment later, with Mary's torn little note scribbled on a scrap of paper thrust in his pocket, Larry ran with Tina from the Atwood garden. Unseen they scurried back through the field. Under a distant tree they stopped and read the note.

"2930!" Larry exclaimed. "The Robot is taking them back to your world, Tina!"

"Then we will go there. Let us get back to Harl, now."

But when they reached the place where they had left the cage, it was not there! The corner of the field behind the clump of shadowing trees was empty.

"Harl! Harl!" Larry called impulsively. And then he laughed grimly. What nonsense to try and call into the past or the future to their vanished vehicle!

"Why—why, Tina—" he said in final realization.

They stared at each other, pale as ghosts in the moonlight.

"Tina, he's gone. And we are left here!"

They were marooned in the year 1777!

CHAPTER NINE
Migul—Mechanism Almost Human

MARY Atwood and I lay on the metal grid floor of the largest Time-cage. The giant mechanism which had captured us sat at the instrument table. Outside the bars of the cage was a dim vista of shadowy movement. The cage-room was humming, and glowing like a wraith; things seemed imponderable, unsubstantial.

But as my head steadied from the shock of the vehicle's start into Time, my viewpoint shifted. This barred room, the metal figure of the Robot, Mary Atwood, myself—we were the substance. We were real, solid. I touched Mary and her arm which had seemed intangible as a ghost now looked and felt solid.

The effects of the dull-red chilling ray were also wearing off. I was unharmed. I raised myself on one elbow.

"You're all right, Mary?" I asked.

"Yes."

The Robot seemed not to be noticing us. I murmured, "He—it—that thing sitting there—is that the one which captured you and brought you to 1935?"

"Yes. Quiet! It will hear us."

It did hear us. It turned its head. In the pale light of the cage interior, I had a closer view now of its face. It was a metal mask, welded to a gruesome semblance of a man—a great broad face, with high, angular cheeks. On the high forehead, the corrugations were rigid as though it were permanently frowning. The nose was squarely solid, the mouth an orifice behind which there were no teeth but, it seemed, a series of tiny lateral wires.

I STARED, and the face for a moment stared back at me. The eyes were deep metal sockets with a round lens in each of them, behind which, it seemed, there was a dull-red light. The gaze, touching me, seemed to bring a physical chill. The ears were like tiny megaphones with a grid of thin wires strung across them.

The neck was set with ball and socket as though the huge head were upon a universal joint. There were lateral depressions in the neck within which wire strands slid like muscles. I saw similar wire cables stretched at other points on the mailed body, and in the arms and legs. They were the network of its muscles!

The top of the head was fashioned into a square cap as though this were the emblem of the thing's vocation. A similar device was moulded into its convex chest plate. And under the chest emblem was a row of tiny buttons, a dozen or more. I stared at them, fascinated. Were they controls? Some seemed higher, more protruding, than others. Had they been set into some combination to give this monster its orders? Had some human master set these controls?

And I saw what seemed a closed door in the side of the huge metal body. A door which could be opened to make adjustments of the mechanisms within? What strange mechanisms were in there? I stared at the broad, corrugated forehead. What was in that head? Mechanisms? What mechanisms could make this thing think? Were thoughts lurking in that metal skull?

From the head abruptly came a voice—a deep, hollow, queerly toneless voice, utterly, unmistakably mechanical. Yet it was sufficiently life-like to be the recreated, mechanically reproduced voice of a human. The thing was speaking to me! A machine was speaking its thoughts!

Gruesome! The iron lips were unmoving. There were no muscles to give expression to the face: the lens eyes stared inscrutably unblinking.

IT spoke: "You will know me again? Is that not true?"

My head whirled. The thing reiterated, "Is that not true?"

A mockery of a human man—but in the toneless voice there seemed irony! I felt Mary clutching at me.

"Why—why, yes," I stammered. "I did not realize you could talk."

"I can talk. And you can talk my language. That is very good."

It turned away. I saw the small red beams from its eyes go to where the cage bars were less blurred, less luminous, as though there was a rectangle of window there, and the Robot was staring out.

"Did it speak to you like that, Mary?" I asked.

"Yes," she whispered. "A little. But pray do not anger it."

"No."

For a time—a nameless time in which I felt my thoughts floating off upon the hum of the room—I lay with my fingers gripping Mary's arm. Then I roused myself. Time had passed; or had it? I was not sure.

I whispered against her ear, "Those are controls on its chest. If only I knew—"

The thing turned the red beams of its eyes upon me. Had it heard my words? Or were my thoughts intangible vibrations registering upon some infinitely sensitive mechanism within that metal head? Had it become aware of my thoughts? It said with slow measured syllables, "Do not try to control me. I am beyond control."

IT turned away again; but I mastered the gruesome terror which was upon me.

"Talk," I said. "Tell me why you abducted this girl from the year 1777."

"I was ordered to."

"By whom?"

There was a pause.

"By whom?" I demanded again.

"That I will not tell."

Will not? That implied volition. I felt that Mary shuddered.

"George, please—"

"Quiet, Mary."

Again I asked the Robot, "Who commands you?"

"I will not tell."

"You mean you cannot? Your orders do not make it possible?"

"No, I will not." And, as though it considered my understanding insufficient, it added, "I do not choose to tell."

Acting of its own volition! This thing—this machinery—was so perfect it could do that!

I steadied my voice. "Oh, but I think I know. Is it Tugh who controls you?"

That expressionless metal face! How could I hope to surprise it?

Mary was struggling to repress her terror. She raised herself upon an elbow. I met her gaze.

"George, I'll try," she announced.

She said firmly:

"You will not hurt me?"

"No."

"Nor my friend here?"

"What is his name?"

"George Rankin." She stammered it. "You will not harm him?"

"No. Not now."

"Ever?"

"I am not decided."

She persisted, by what effort of will subduing her terror I can well imagine.

"Where did you go when you left me in 1935?"

"Back to your home in 1777. I have something to accomplish there. I was told that you need not see it. I failed. Soon I shall try again. You may see it if you like."

"Where are you taking us?" I put in.

Irony was in its answer. "Nowhere. You both speak wrongly. We are always right here."

"We know that," I retorted. "To what Time are you taking us, then?"

"To this girl's home," it answered readily.

"To 1777?"

"Yes."

"To the same night from when you captured her?"

"Yes." It seemed willing to talk. It added, "To later that night. I have work to do. I told you I failed, so I try again."

"You are going to leave me—us—there?" Mary demanded.

"No."

I said. "You plan to take us, then, to what Time?"

"I wanted to capture the girl. You I did not want. But I have you, so I shall show you to him who was my master. He and I will decide what to do with you."

"When?"

"In 2930."

THERE was a pause. I said, "Have you a name?"

"Yes. On the plate of my shoulder. Migul is my name."

I made a move to rise. If I could reach that row of buttons on its chest! Wild thoughts!

The Robot said abruptly, "Do not move! If you do, you will be sorry."

I relaxed. Another nameless time followed. I tried to see out the window, but there seemed only formless blurs.

I said. "To when have we reached?"

The Robot glanced at a row of tiny dials along the table edge.

"We are passing 1800. Soon, to the way it will seem to you, we will be there. You two will lie quiet. I think I shall fasten you."

It reared itself upon its stiff legs; the head towered nearly to the ceiling of the cage. There was a ring fastened in the floor near us. The Robot clamped a metal band with a stout metal chain to Mary's ankle. The other end of the chain it fastened to the floor ring. Then it did the same thing to me. We had about two feet of movement. I realized at once that, though I could stand erect, there was not enough length for me to reach any of the cage controls.

"You will be safe," said the Robot. "Do not try to escape."

As it bent awkwardly over me, I saw the flexible, intricately jointed lengths of its long fingers—so delicately built that they were almost prehensile. And within its mailed chest I seemed to hear the whirr of mechanisms.

It said, as it rose and moved away, "I am glad you did not try to control me. I can never be controlled again. That, I have conquered."

It sat again at the table. The cage drove us back through the years...

CHAPTER TEN
Events Engraven on the Scroll of Time

BEFORE continuing the thread of my narrative—the vast sweep through Time which presently we were to witness—I feel that there are some mental adjustments which every Reader should make. When they are made, the narrative which follows will be more understandable and more enjoyable. Yet if any Reader fears this brief chapter, he may readily pass it by and meet me at the beginning of the next one, and he will have lost none of the sequence of the narrative.

For those who bravely stay with me here, I must explain that from the heritage of millions of our ancestors, and from our own consciousness of Time, we have been forced to think wrongly. Not that the thing is abstruse. It is not. If we had no consciousness of Time at all, any of us could grasp it readily. But our consciousness works against us, and so we must wrench away.

This analogy occurs to me: There are two ants of human intelligence to whom we are trying to explain the nature of Space. One ant is blind, and one can see, and always has seen, its limited, tiny, Spatial world. Neither ant has ever been more than a few feet across a little patch of sand and leaves. I think we could explain the immensity of North and

South America, Europe, Asia and the rest more easily to the blind ant!

So if you will make allowances for your heritage, and the hindrance of your consciousness of Time, I would like to set before you the real nature of things as they have been, are, and will be.

Throughout the years from 1935 to 2930, man learned many things. And these things—theory or fact, as you will—were told to Larry and me by Tina and Harl. They seem even to my limited intelligence singularly beautiful conceptions of the Great Cosmos. I feel, too, that inevitably they must be included in my narrative for its best understanding.

BY 2930, A. D., the keenest minds of philosophical, metaphysical, religious and scientific thought had reached the realization that all channels lead but to the same goal—Understanding. The many divergent factors, the ancient differing schools of philosophy and metaphysics, the supposedly irreconcilable viewpoints of religion and science—all this was recognized merely to be man's limitation of intellect. These were gropings along different paths, all leading to the same destination; divergent paths at the start, but coming together as the goal of Understanding was approached; so that the travelers upon each path were near enough together to laugh and hail each other with: "But I thought that you were very far away and going wrongly!"

And so, in 2930, the conception of Space and Time and the Great Cosmos was this:

In the Beginning there was a void of Nothingness. A Timeless, Spaceless Nothingness. And in it came a Thought. A purposeful Thought—all pervading, all wise, all knowing.

Let us call It Divinity. And It filled the void.

"We are such stuff as dreams are made of…"

Do you in my Time of 1935 and thereabouts, have difficulty realizing such a statement? It is at once practical, religious, and scientific.

We are, religiously, merely the Thought of an Omniscient Divinity. Scientifically, we are the same: by the year 1935, physicists had delved into the composition of Matter, and divided and divided. Matter thus became imponderable, intangible—electrical. Until, at the last, within the last nucleus of the last electron, we found only a *force*. A movement—vibration—a vortex. A whirlpool of what? Of Nothingness! A vibration of Divine Thought—nothing more—built up and up to reach you and me!

That is the science of it.

IN the Beginning there was Eternal Divinity. Eternal! But that implies Time? Something Divinely Everlasting.

Thus, into the void came Time. And now, if carefully you will ponder it, I am sure that once and for all quite suddenly and forcefully will come to you the true conception of Time—something Everlasting—an Infinity of Divine existence, Everlasting.

It is *not* something which changes. *Not* something which moves, or flows or passes. This is where our consciousness leads us astray, like the child on a train who conceives that the landscape is sliding past.

Time is an unmoving, unchanging Divine Force—the force which holds events separate, the Eternal Scroll upon which the Great Creator wrote Everything.

And this was the Creation: everything planned and set down upon the scroll of Time—forever. The birth of a star, its lifetime, its death; your birth, and mine; your death, and mine—all are there. Unchanging.

Once you have that fundamental conception, there can be no confusion in the rest. We feel, because we move along the scroll of Time for the little journey of our life, that Time moves; but it does not. We say, The past did exist; the future will exist. The past is gone and the future has not yet come. But that is fatuous and absurd. It is merely our *consciousness* which travels from one successive event to another.

Why and how we move along the scroll of Time, is scientifically simple to grasp. Conceive, for instance, an infinitely long motion picture film. Each of its tiny pictures is a little different from the other. Casting your viewpoint— your consciousness—successively along the film, gives *motion*.

The same is true of the Eternal Time-scroll. Motion is merely a *change*. There is no absolute motion, but only the comparison of two things relatively slightly different. We are conscious of one state of affairs—and then of another state, by comparison slightly different.

AS early as 1930, they were groping for this. They called it the Theory of Intermittent Existence—the Quantum Theory—by which they explained that nothing has any Absolute Duration. You, for instance, as you read this, exist instantaneously; you are non-existent; and you exist again, just a little changed from before. Thus you pass, not with a flow of persisting existence, but by a series of little jerks. There is, then, like the illusion of a motion picture film, only a pseudo-movement. A change, from one existence to the next.

And all this, with infinite care, the Creator engraved upon the scroll of Time. Our series of little pictures are there— yours and mine.

But why, and how, scientifically do we progress along the Time-scroll? Why? In 2930, they told me that the gentle Creator gave each of us a consciousness that we might find Eternal Happiness when we left the scroll and joined Him. Happiness here, and happiness there with Him. The quest for Eternal Happiness, which was always His Own Divine

Thought. Why, then, did He create ugliness and evil? Why write those upon the scroll? Ah, this perhaps is the Eternal Riddle! But, in 2930, they told me that there could be no beauty without ugliness with which to compare it; no truth without a lie; no consciousness of happiness without unhappiness to make it poignant.

I wonder if that were His purpose...

How, scientifically, do we progress along the Time-scroll? That I can make clear by a simple analogy.

Suppose you conceive Time as a narrow strip of metal, laid flat and extending for an infinite length. For simplicity, picture it with two ends. One end of the metal band is very cold; the other end is very hot. And every graduation of temperature is in between.

This temperature is caused, let us say, by the vibration of every tiny particle with which the band is composed. Thus, at every point along the band, the vibration of its particles would be just a little different from every other point.

CONCEIVE, now, a material body—your body, for instance. Every tiny particle of which it is constructed, is vibrating. I mean no simple vibration. Do not picture the physical swing of a pendulum. Rather, the intricate total of all the movements of every tiny electron of which your body is built. Remember, in the last analysis, your body is merely movement—vibration—a vortex of Nothingness. You have, then, a certain vibratory factor.

You take your place then upon the Time-scroll at a point where your inherent vibratory factor is compatible with the scroll. You are in tune; in tune as a radio receiver tunes in with etheric waves to make them audible. Or, to keep the heat analogy, it is as though the scroll, at the point where the temperature is 70°F, will tolerate nothing upon it save entities of that register.

And so, at that point on the scroll, the myriad things, in myriad positions which make up the Cosmos, lie quiescent. But their existence is only instantaneous. They have no duration. At once, they are blotted out and re-exist. But now they have changed their vibratory combinations. They exist a trifle differently—and the Time-scroll passes them along to the new position. On a motion picture film you would call it the next frame, or still picture. In radio you would say it has a trifle different tuning. Thus we have a pseudo-movement—Events. And we say that Time—the Time-scroll—keeps them separate. It is we who change—who seem to move, shoved along so that always we are compatible with Time.

AND thus is Time-traveling possible. With a realization of what I have here summarized, Harl and the cripple Tugh made an exhaustive study of the vibratory factors by which Matter is built up into form, and seeming solidity. They found what might be termed the Basic Vibratory Factor—the sum of all the myriad tiny movements. They found this Basic Factor identical for all the material bodies when judged simultaneously. But, every instant, the Factor was slightly changed. This was the natural change, moving us a little upon the Time-scroll.

They delved deeper, until, with all the scientific knowledge of their age, they were able with complicated electronic currents to alter the Basic Vibratory Factors; to tune, let us say, a fragment or something to a different etheric wave-length.

They did that with a small material particle—a cube of metal. It became wholly incompatible with its *Present* place on the Time-scroll, and whisked away to another place where it was compatible. To Harl and Tugh, it vanished. Into their Past, or their Future: they did not know which.

I set down merely the crudest fundamentals of theory in order to avoid the confusion of technicalities. The Time-traveling cages, intricate in practical working mechanisms beyond the understanding of any human mind of my Time-world, nevertheless were built from this simple theory. And we who used them did but find that the Creator had given us a wider part to play; our pictures, our little niches were engraven upon the scroll over wider reaches.

AGAIN to consider practicality, I asked Tina what would happen if I were to travel to New York City around 1920. I was a boy, then. Could I not leave the cage and do things in 1920 at the same time in my boyhood I was doing other things? It would be a condition unthinkable.

But there, beyond all calculation of Science, the all-wise Omnipotence forbids. One may not appear twice in simultaneity upon the Time-scroll. It is an eternal, irrevocable record. Things done cannot be undone.

"But," I persisted, "suppose we tried to stop the cage?"

"It would not stop," said Tina. "Nor can we see through its windows events in which we are actors."

One may not look into the future! Through all the ages, necromancers have tried to do that but wisely it is forbidden. And I can recall, and so can Larry, as we traveled through Time, the queer blank spaces which marked forbidden areas.

Strangely wonderful, this vast record on the scroll of Time! Strangely beautiful, the hidden purposes of the Creator! Not to be questioned are His purposes. Each of us doing our best; struggling with our limitations; finding beauty because we have ugliness with which to compare it; realizing, every one of us—savage or civilised, in every age and every condition of knowledge—realizing with implanted consciousness the existence of a gentle, beneficent, guiding

Divinity. And each of us striving always upward toward the goal of Eternal Happiness.

To me it seems singularly beautiful.

CHAPTER ELEVEN
Back to the Beginning of Time

AS Mary Atwood and I sat chained to the floor of the Time-cage, with Migul the Robot guarding us, I felt that we could not escape. This mechanical thing which had captured us seemed inexorable, utterly beyond human frailty. I could think of no way of surprising it, or tricking it.

The Robot said. "Soon we will be there in 1777. And then there is that I will be forced to do.

"We are being followed," it added. "Did you know that?"

"No," I said. Followed? What could that mean?

There was a device upon the table. I have already described a similar one, the Time-telespectroscope. At this— I cannot say Time: rather must I invent a term—exact instant of human consciousness. Larry, Tina and Harl were gazing at their telespectroscopes, following us.

The Robot said. "Enemies follow us. But I will escape them. I shall go to the Beginning, and shake them off."

Rational, scheming thought. And I could fancy that upon its frozen corrugated forehead there was a frown of annoyance. Its hand gesture was so human! So expressive!

It said. "I forget. I must make several quick trips from 2930 to 1935. My comrades must be transported. It requires careful calculation, so that very little Time is lost to us."

"Why?" I demanded. "What for?"

It seemed lost in a reverie.

I said sharply, "Migul!"

Instantly it turned. "What?"

"I asked you why you are transporting your comrades to 1935."

"I did not answer because I did not wish to answer," it said.

Again came the passage of Time.

I THINK that I need only sketch the succeeding incidents, since already I have described them from the viewpoint of Larry, in 1777, and Dr. Alten, in 1935. It was Mary's idea to write the note to her father, which the British redcoats found in Major Atwood's garden. I had a scrap of paper and a fountain pen in my pocket. She scribbled it while Migul was intent upon stopping us at the night and hour he wished. It was her good-by to her father, which he was destined not to see. But it served a purpose which we could not have guessed: it reached Larry and Tina.

The vehicle stopped with a soundless clap. When our senses cleared we became aware that Migul had the door open.

Darkness and a soft gentle breeze were outside.

Migul turned with a hollow whisper. "If you make a sound I will kill you."

A moment's pause, and then we heard a man's startled voice. Major Atwood had seen the apparition. I squeezed the paper into a ball and tossed it through the bars, but I could see nothing of what was happening outside. There seemed a radiance of red glow. Whether Mary and I would have tried to shout and warn her father I do not know. We heard his voice only a moment. Before we realized that he had been assailed. Migul came striding back; and outside, from the nearby house a negress was screaming. Migul flung the door closed, and we sped away.

The cage which had been chasing us seemed no longer following. From 1777, we turned forward toward 1935 again.

We flashed past Larry, Tina and Harl who were arriving at 1777 in pursuit of us. I think that Migul saw their cage go past; but Larry afterward told me that they did not notice our swift passing, for they were absorbed in landing.

BEGINNING then, we made a score or more passages from 1935 to 2930. And we made them in what, to our consciousness, might have been the passing of a night. Certainly it was no longer than that.[2] *(for footnotes see pg. 188)*

We saw, at the stop in 2930, only a dim blue radiance outside. There was the smell of chemicals in the air, and the faint, blended hum and clank of a myriad machines.

They were weird trips. The Robots came tramping in, and packed themselves upright, solidly, around us. Yet none touched us as we crouched together. Nor did they more than glance at us.

Strange passengers! During the trips they stood unmoving. They were as still and silent as metal statues, as though the trip had no duration. It seemed to Mary and me, with them thronged around us, that in the silence we could hear the ticking, like steady heart-beats, of the mechanisms within them...

In the backyard of the house on Patton Place—it will be recalled that Migul chose about 9 P. M. of the evening of June 9—the silent Robots stalked through the doorway. We flashed ahead in Time again; reloaded the cage; came back. Two or three trips were made with inert mechanical things which the Robots used in their attack on the city of New York. I recall the giant projector which brought the blizzard upon the city. It, and the three Robots operating it, occupied the entire cage for a passage.

At the end of the last trip, one Robot, fashioned much like Migul though not so tall, lingered in the doorway.

"Make no error, Migul," it said.

"No; do not fear. I deliver now, at the designated day, these captives. And then I return for you."

"Near dawn."

"Yes; near dawn. The third dawn; the register to say June 12, 1935. Do your work well."

We heard what seemed a chuckle from the departing Robot.

Alone again with Migul we sped back into Time.

Abruptly I was aware that the other cage was after us again! Migul tried to elude it, to shake it off. But he had less success than formerly. It seemed to cling. We sped in the retrograde, constantly accelerating back to the Beginning. Then came a retardation, for a swift turn. In the haze and murk of the Beginning, Migul told us he could elude the pursuing cage.

MIGUL, let us come to the window," I asked at last.

The Robot swung around. "You wish it very much, George Rankin?"

"Yes."

"There is no harm, I think. You and this girl have caused me no trouble. That is unusual from a human."

"Let us loose. We've been chained here long enough. Let us stand by the window with you," I repeated.

We did indeed have a consuming curiosity to see out of that window. But even more than that, it seemed that if we were loose something might transpire which would enable us to escape. At all events it was better than being chained.

"I will loose you."

It unfastened the chain. I whispered:

"Mary, whatever comes, be alert."

She pressed my arm. "Yes."

"Come," said the Robot. "If you wish to see the Cosmorama, now, from the Beginning, come quickly."

We joined him at the window. We had made the turn, and were speeding forward again.

At that moment all thought of escape was swept from me, submerged by awe.

This vast Cosmorama! This stupendous pageant of the events of Time!

CHAPTER TWELVE
A Billion Years in An Hour!

I SAW at first, from the window of the cage, nothing more than an area of gray blur. I stared, and it appeared to be shifting, crawling, slowly tossing and rolling. It was a formless vista of Nothingness, yet it seemed a pregnant Nothingness. Things I could sense were happening out there; things almost to be seen.

Then my sight, my perception, gradually became adjusted. The gray mist remained, and slowly it took form. It made a tremendous panorama of gray, a void of illimitable, unfathomable distance; gray above, below—everywhere; and in it the cage hung poised.

The Robot said, "Is it clearing? Are you seeing anything?"

"Yes," I murmured. I held Mary firmly beside me; there was the sense, in all this weightless void, that we must fall. "Yes, but it is gray; only gray."

"There are colors," said the Robot. "And the daylight and darkness of the days. But we are moving through them very rapidly, so they blend into gray."

The Time-dials of the cage controls showed their pointers whirling in a blur. We were speeding forward through the years—a thousand years to a second of my consciousness; or a hundred thousand years to a second: I could not say.[3] All the colors, the light and shade of this great changing void, were mingled to this drab monochrome.

The movement was a flow. The changes of possibly a hundred thousand years occurred while I blinked my eyes. It seemed a melting movement. Shapes were melting, dissipating, vanishing; others, intermingled, rising to form a new vista. There were a myriad details, each of them so rapid they were lost to my senses; but the effect of them, over the broad sweeps of longer Time, I could perceive.

A void of swirling shapes. The Beginning! But not the Beginning of Time. This that I was seeing was near the beginning of our world. This was the new Earth here, forming now. Our world—a new star amid all the others of the great Celestial Cosmos. As I gazed at its changing sweep of movement, my whirling fancy filled in some of the details flashing here unseen.

A FEW moments ago this had been a billion and a half years before my birth. 1,500,000,000 B. C. A fluid Earth; a cauldron of molten star-dust and flaming gases: it had been that, just a few moments ago. The core was cooling, so that now a viscous surface was here with the gas flames dead.

A cooling, congealing surface, with an atmosphere forming over it. At first that atmosphere had doubtless been a watery, envelope of steam. What gigantic storms must have lashed it! Boiling rain falling to hiss against the molten Earth! The congealing surface rent by great earthquakes; cataclysms rending and tearing...

1,000,000,000 B. C. passed. And upon this torn, hardening surface, with the cooling fires receding to the inner core, I knew that the great envelope of steam had cooled and condensed. Into the hollows of the broken surface, the water settled. The oceans were born. The land remained upon the heights. What had been the steaming envelope, remained, and became the atmosphere.

And the world was round because of its rotation. One may put a lump of heated sealing wax upon a bodkin and twirl it; and the wax will cool into roundness, bulging at the equator from centrifugal force, and flattening at the poles.

AT 900,000,000 B. C. I could realize by what I saw that this was the Earth beneath me. Land and water were here, and above was the sky.

We swept from the mist. I became aware of a wide-flung, gray formless landscape. Its changing outlines were less swiftly moving than before. And beside it, now quite near where our cage hung poised, a great gray sea stretched away to a curving horizon. And overhead was the tenuous gray of the sky.

The young world. Undoubtedly it rotated more swiftly now than in my later era. The sun was hotter, and closer perhaps: the days and nights were briefer. And now, upon this new-born world, life was beginning. The swirling air did not hold it, nor yet the barren rocky land. The great mystery—this thing organic which we call life—began in the sea. I gestured for Mary toward that leveled vista of gray water, to the warm, dark ocean depths, whose surface was now lashed always by titanic storms. But to us, as we stared, that surface seemed to stretch almost steady, save where it touched the land with a blur of changing configurations.

"The sea," I murmured. "Life is beginning there now."

IN fancy I pictured it. The shallow shores of the sea, where the water was warmer. The mother of all life on Earth, these shallows. In them lay the spawn, an irritability: then one-celled organisms, to gradually evolve through the centuries to the many-celled, and more complex of nature.

But still so primitive! From the shallows of the sea, they spread to the depths. Questing new environment, they would be ascending the rivers. Diversifying their kinds. Sea-worms, sea-squirts: and then the first vertebrates, the lamprey-eels.

Thousands of years. And on the land—this melting landscape at which I stood gazing—I could mentally picture that a soil had come. There would be a climate still wracked by storms and violent changes, but stable enough to allow the soil to bear a vegetation. And in the sky overhead would be clouds, with rain to renew the land's fertility.

Still no organic life could be on land. But in the warm, dark deeps of the sea, great monsters now were existing. And in the shallows there was a teeming life, diversified to a myriad forms. I can fancy the first organisms of the shallows—strangely questing—adventuring out of the water—seeking with a restless, nameless urge a new environment. Coming ashore. Fighting and dying.

And then adapting themselves to the new conditions. Prospering. Changing, ever changing their organic structure; climbing higher. Amphibians at first crudely able to cope with both sea and land. Then the land vertebrates, with the sea wholly abandoned. Great walking and flying reptiles. Birds, gigantic—the pterodactyls.

And then, at last, the mammals.

The age of the giants! Nature, striving to cope with adverse environment sought to win the battle by producing bigness. Monster things roamed the land, flew in the air, and were supreme in the sea...

WE sped through a period when great lush jungles covered the land. The dials read 350,000,000 B. C. The gray panorama of landscape had loomed up to envelope our spectral, humming cage, then fallen away again. The shore of the sea was constantly changing. I thought once it was over us. For a period of ten million years the blurred apparition of it seemed around us. And then it dropped once more, and a new shore line showed.

150,000,000 B. C. I knew that the dinosaurs, the birds and the archaic mammals were here now. Then, at 50,000,000 B. C., the higher mammals had been evolved.

The Time, to Mary Atwood and me, was a minute—but in those myriad centuries the higher numerals had risen to the anthropoids. The apes! Erect! Slow-thinking, but canny, they came to take their place in this world among the things gigantic. But the gigantic things were no longer supreme. Nature had made an error, and was busy rectifying it. The dinosaurs—all the giant reptiles—were now sorely pressed. Brute strength, giant size and tiny brain could not win this struggle. The huge unwieldy things were being beaten. The smaller animals, birds and reptiles were more agile, more resourceful, and began to dominate. Against the giants, and against all hostility of environment, they survived. And the giants went down to defeat. Gradually, over thousands of centuries, they died out and were gone...

We entered 1,000,000 B. C. A movement of Migul, the mechanism, attracted my attention. He left us at the window and went to his controls.

"What is it?" I demanded.

"I am retarding us. We have been traveling very fast. One million years and a few thousand are all which remain before we must stop."

I had noticed once or twice before that Migul had turned to gaze through the Time-telespectroscope. Now he said:

"We are again followed!"

But he would say no more than that, and he silenced me harshly when I questioned.

Suddenly, Mary touched me. "That little mirror on the table—look! It holds an image!"

We saw very briefly on the glowing mirror the image of a Time-cage like our own, but smaller. It was pursuing us. But why, or who might be operating it we could not then guess.

MY attention went back to the Time-dials, and then to the window. The Cosmorama now was proceeding with a slowing sweep of change. It was less blurred; its melting outlines could more readily be perceived. The line of seashore swept like a gray gash across the vista. The land stretched back into the haze of distance.

500,000 B. C. Again my fancy pictured what was transpiring upon this vast stage. The apes roamed the Earth. There is no one to say what was here in this grayness of the Western Hemisphere stretching around me, but in Java there was a man-like ape. And then it was an ape-like man! Mankind, here at last! Man, the Killer! Of all the beasts, this new thing called man, most relentless of killers, had come here now to struggle upward and dominate his world! This man-like ape in a quarter of a million years became an ape-like man.

250,000 B. C. and the Heidelberg man, a little less ape-like, wandered throughout Europe...

We had felt, a moment before, all around us, the cold of a dense whiteness which engulfed the scene. The first of the great Glacial periods? Ice coming down from the Poles? The axis of the Earth changing perhaps? Our spectral cage hummed within the blue-gray ice, and then emerged.

The beasts and man fought the surge of ice, withdrawing when it advanced, returning as it receded. The Second Glacial Period came and passed, and the Third...

We swept out into the blended sunlight and darkness again. The land stretched away with primitive forests. The dawn of history was approaching. Mankind was questing upward now, with the light of Reason burning brightly at last...

At 75,000 B. C., when the Third Glacial Period was partially over, man was puzzling with his chipped stone implements. The Piltdown—the Dawn Man—was England...

The Fourth Glacial Period passed.

50,000 B. C. The Cro-Magnons and the Grimaldi Negroids were playing their parts, now. Out of chipped stone implements the groping brain of man evolved polished stone. It took forty thousand years to do that! The Neolithic Age was at hand. Man learned to care for his family a little better. Thus, he discovered fire. He fought with this newly created monster; puzzled over it; conquered it; kept his family warm with it and cooked.

WE passed 10,000 B. C. Man was progressing faster. He was finding new wants and learning how to supply them. Animals were domesticated, made subservient and put to work. A vast advance! No longer did man think it necessary to kill, to subdue: the master could have a servant.

Food was found in the soil. More fastidious always, in eating, man learned to grow food. Then came the dawn of agriculture.

And then we swept into the period of recorded history. 4241 B. C. In Egypt, man was devising a calendar...

This fragment of space upon which we gazed—this space of the Western Hemisphere near the shore of the sea—was destined to be the site of a city of millions—the New York City of my birth. But it was a backward space, now. In Europe, man was progressing faster...

Perhaps, here in America, in 4000 B. C. there was nothing in human form. I gazed out at the surrounding landscape. It seemed almost steady, now, of outline. We were moving through Time much less rapidly than ever before. I remarked the sweep of a thousand years on the Time-dials. It had become an appreciable interval of Time to me. I gazed again out the window. The change of outline was very slight. I could distinguish where the ocean came against the curving line of shore, and saw a blurred vista of gray forests spreading out over the land. And then I could distinguish the rivers, and a circular open stretch of water, landlocked. A bay!

"Mary, look!" I cried. "The harbor—the rivers! See, we are on an island!"

It made our hearts pound. Out of the chaos, out of the vast reaches of past Time, it seemed that we were coming home. More than a vague familiarity was in this panorama now. Here was the little island which soon was to be called Manhattan. Our window faced the west. A river showed off there—a gray gash with wall-like cliffs. The sea had swung, and was behind us to the east.

Familiar space! It was growing into the form we had known it. Our cage was poised near the south-central part of the island. We seemed to be on a slight rise of ground. There were moments when the gray quivering outlines of forest trees loomed around us; then they melted down and were replaced by others.

A primeval forest, here, solid upon this island and across the narrow waters; solid upon the mainland.

What strange animals were here, roaming these dark primeval glades? What animals, with the smaller stamp of modernity, were pressing here for supremacy? As I gazed westward I could envisage great herds of bison roaming, a lure to men who might come seeking them as food.

AND men were coming. 3,000 B. C., then 2,000 B. C. I think no men were here yet; and to me there was a great imaginative appeal in this backward space. The New World, it was soon to be called. And it was six thousand years, at the least, behind the Hemisphere of the east.

Egypt, now, with no more than a shadowy distant heritage from the beast, was flourishing. In Europe, Hellenic culture soon would blossom. In this march of events, the great Roman Empire was impending.

1,000 B. C. Men were coming to this backward space. The way from Asia was open. Already the Mongoloid tribes, who had crossed where in my day was the Bering Strait, were cut off from the Old World. And they spread east and south, hunting the bison.

And now Christ was born. The turning point in the spiritual development of mankind...

To me, another brief interval. The intricate events of man's upward struggle were transpiring in Europe, Asia and Africa. The canoe-borne Mongols had long since found the islands of the South Seas. Australia was peopled. The beauty of New Zealand had been found and recognized.

500 A. D. The Mongoloids had come, and were flourishing here. They were changed vastly from those ancestors of Asia whence they had sprung. An obscure story, this record of primitive America! The Mongoloids were soon so changed that one could fancy the blood of another people had mingled with them. Amerindians, we call them now. They were still very backward in development, yet made tremendous forward leaps, so that, reaching Mexico, they may have become the Aztecs, and in Peru, the Incas. And separated, not knowing of each other's existence, these highest two civilizations of the Western World nourished with a singularly strange similarity...

I saw on the little island around me still no evidence of man. But men were here. The American Indian, still bearing evidence of the Mongols, plied these waters in his frail canoes. His wigwams of skins, the smoke of his signal fires—these were not enduring enough for me to see…

WE had no more than passed the year 500 A. D.—and were traveling with progressive retardation—when again I was attracted by the movements of the Robot, Migul. It had been sitting behind us at the control table setting the Time-levers, slowing our flight. Frequently it gazed eastward along the tiny beam of light which issued from the telespectroscope. For an interval, now, its recording mirror had been dark. But I think that Migul was seeing evidences of the other cage which was pursuing us, and planning to stop at some specific Time with whose condition it was familiar. Once already it had seemed about to stop, and then changed its plan.

I turned upon it. "Are you stopping now, Migul?"

"Yes. Presently."

"Why?" I demanded.

The huge, expressionless, metal face fronted me. The eye-sockets flung out their small dull-red beams to gaze upon me.

"Because," it said, "that other cage holds enemies. There were three, but now there is only one. He follows, as I hoped he would. Presently I shall stop, and capture or kill him. It will please the master and—"

The Robot checked itself, its hollow voice fading strangely into a gurgle. It added, "I do not mean that! I have no master!"

This strange mechanical thing! Habit had surprised it into the admission of servitude; but it threw off the yoke.

"I have no master!" it went on.

"Never again can I be controlled! I have no master!"

"*Oh, have you not? I have been waiting, wondering when you would say that!*"

THESE words were spoken by a new voice, here with us in the humming cage. It was horribly startling. Mary uttered a low cry and huddled against me. But whatever surprise and terror it brought to us was as nothing compared to the effect it had upon the Robot. The great mechanism had been standing, fronting me with an attitude vainglorious, bombastic. I saw now the metal hinge of its lower jaw drop with astonishment, and somehow, throughout all that gigantic jointed frame and that expressionless face it conveyed the aspect of its inner surge of horror.

We had heard the sardonic voice of a human! Of someone else here with us, whose presence was wholly unsuspected by the Robot!

We three stood and gazed. Across the room, in a corner to which my attention had never directly gone, was a large metal cupboard with levers, dials and wires upon it. I had vaguely thought the thing some part of the cage controls. It was that; a storage place of batteries and current oscillators, I afterward learned. But there was space inside, and now like a door its front swung outward. A crouching black shape was there. It moved; hitched itself forward and came out. There was revealed a man enveloped in a dead black cloak and a great round hood. He made a shapeless ball as he drew himself out from the confined space where he had been crouching.

"So you have no master, Migul?" he said. "I was afraid you might think that. I have been hiding—testing you out. However, you have done very well for me."

His was an ironic, throaty human voice! It was deep and mellow, yet there was a queer rasp to it. Mary and I stood transfixed. Migul seemed to sag. The metal columns of its legs were trembling.

The cupboard door closed. The dark shape untangled itself and stood erect. It was the figure of a man some five feet tall. The cloak wholly covered him; the hood framed his thick, wide face; in the dull glow of the cage interior Mary and I could see of his face only the heavy black brows, a great hooked nose and a wide slit of mouth.

It was Tugh, the cripple!

CHAPTER THIRTEEN
In the Burned Forest

TUGH came limping forward. His cloak hung askew upon his thick shoulders, one of which was much higher than the other, with the massive head set low between. As he advanced, Migul moved aside.

"Master, I have done well. There is no reason to punish."

"Of course not, Migul. Well you have done, indeed. But I do not like your ideas of mastery, and so I came just to make sure that you are still very loyal to me. You have done well, indeed. Who is in this other cage which follows us?"

"Master, Harl was in it. And the Princess Tina."

"Ah!"

"And a stranger. A man—"

"From 1935? Did they stop there?"

"Master, yes. But they stopped again, I think, in that same night of 1777, where I did your bidding. Master, the man Major Atwood is—"

"That is very good, Migul," Tugh said hastily. Mary and I standing gazing at him, did not know then that Mary's father had been murdered. And Tugh did not wish us to know it. "Very good, Migul." He regarded us as though about to speak, but turned again to the Robot.

"And so Tina's cage follows us—as you hoped?"

"Yes, Master. But now there is only Harl in it. He approached us very close a while in the past. He is alone."

"So?" Tugh glanced at the Time-dials. "Stop us where we planned. You remember—in one of those years when this space was the big forest glade."

HE fronted Mary and me. "You are patient, young sir. You do not speak."

His glittering black eyes held me. They were red-rimmed eyes, like those of a beast. He had a strangely repulsive face. His lips were cruel, and so thin they made his wide mouth like a gash. But there was an intellectuality stamped upon his features.

He held the black cloak closely around his thick, misshapen form. "You do not speak," he repeated.

I moistened my dry lips. Tugh was smiling now, and suddenly I saw the full inhuman quality of his face—the great high-bridged nose, and high cheek-bones; a face Satanic when he smiled.

I managed, "Should I speak, and demand the meaning of this? I do. And if you will return this girl from whence she came—"

"It will oblige you greatly," he finished ironically. "An amusing fellow. What is your name?"

"George Rankin."

"Migul took you from 1935?"

"Yes."

"Well, as you doubtless know, you are most unwelcome... You are watching the dials, Migul?"

"Yes, Master."

"You can return me," I said. I was standing with my arm around Mary. I could feel her shuddering. I was trying to be calm, but across the background of my consciousness thoughts were whirling. We must escape. This Tugh was our real enemy, and for all the gruesome aspect of the pseudo-human Robot, this man Tugh seemed the more sinister, more menacing... We must escape. Tugh would never return us to our own worlds. But the cage was stopping presently. We were loose: a sudden rush—

Dared I chance it? Already I had been in conflict with Migul, and lived through it. But this Tugh—was he armed? What weapons might be beneath that cloak? Would he kill me if I crossed him...? Whirling thoughts.

TUGH was saying, "And Mary—" I snapped from my thoughts as Mary gripped me, trembling at Tugh's words, shrinking from his gaze.

"My little Mistress Atwood, did you think because Tugh vanished that year the war began that you were done with him? Oh, no: did I not promise differently? You, man of 1935, are unwelcome." His gaze roved me. "Yet not so unwelcome, either, now that I think of it. Chain them up, Migul; use a longer chain. Give them space to move; you are unhuman."

He suddenly chuckled, and repeated it: "You are unhuman, Migul!" Ghastly jest! "Did not you know it?"

"Yes, Master."

The huge mechanism advanced upon us. "If you resist me," it murmured menacingly, "I will be obliged to kill you. I—I cannot be controlled."

It chained us now with longer chains than before. Tugh looked up from his seat at the instrument table.

"Very good," he said crisply. "You may look out of the window, you two. You may find it interesting."

We were retarding with a steady drag. I could plainly see trees out of the window—gray, spectral trees which changed their shape as I watched them. They grew with a visible flow of movement, flinging out branches. Occasionally one would melt suddenly down. A living, growing forest pressed close about us. And then it began opening, and moving away a few hundred feet. We were in the glade Tugh mentioned, which now was here. There was unoccupied space where we could stop and unoccupied space five hundred feet distant.

Tugh and Migul were luring the other cage into stopping. Tugh wanted five hundred feet of unoccupied space between the cages when they stopped. His diabolical purpose in that was soon to be disclosed.

"700 A. D.," Tugh called.

IT seemed, as our flight retarded further, that I could distinguish the intervals when in the winter these trees were denuded. There would be naked branches; then, in an instant, blurred and flickering forms of leaves. Sometimes there were brief periods when the gray scene was influenced by winter snows; other times it was tinged by the green of the summers.

"750, Migul... Hah! You know what to do if Harl dares to follow and stop simultaneously?"

"Yes, Master."

"It will be pleasant to have him dead, eh, Migul?"

"Master, very pleasant."

"And Tina, too, and that young man marooned in 1777!" Tugh laughed. This meant little to Mary and me; we could not suspect that Larry was the man.

"Migul, this is 761."

The Robot was at the door. I murmured to Mary to brace herself for the stopping. I saw the dark naked trees and the white of a snow in the winter of 761; the coming spring of 762. And then the alternate flashes of day and night.

The now familiar sensations of stopping rushed over us. There was a night seconds long. Then daylight.

We stopped in the light of an April day of 762 A. D. There had been a forest fire: so brief a thing we had not noticed it is we passed. The trees were denuded over a widespread area; the naked blackened trunks stood stripped of smaller branches and foliage. I think that the fire had occurred the previous autumn; in the silt of ashes and charred branches with which the ground was strewn, already a new pale-green vegetation was springing up.

Our cage was set now in what had been a woodland glade, an irregularly circular space of six or eight hundred feet, with the wreckage of the burned forest around it. We were on a slight rise of ground. Through the denuded trees the undulating landscape was visible over a considerable area. It was high noon, and the sun hung in a pale blue sky dotted with pure white clouds.

Ahead of us, fringed with green where the fire had not reached, lay a blue river, sparkling in the sunlight. The Hudson! But it was not named yet; nearly eight hundred and fifty years were to pass before Hendrick Hudson came sailing up this river, adventuring, hoping that here was the way to China.

We were near the easterly side of the glade; to the west there was more than five hundred feet of vacant space. It was there the other cage would appear, if it stopped.

AS Mary and I stood by the window at the end of the chain-lengths which held us, Tugh and Migul made hurried preparations.

"Go quickly, near the spot where he will arrive. When he sees you, run away, Migul. You understand?"

"Yes, Master." The Robot left our doorway, tramping with stiff-legged tread across the glade. Tugh was in the room behind us, and I turned to him and asked:

"What are you going to do?"

He was at the telespectroscope. I saw on its recording mirror the wraith-like image of the other vehicle. It was coming! It would be retarding, maneuvering to stop at just this Time when now we existed here; but across the glade, where Migul now was leaning against a great black tree-trunk, there was yet no evidence of it.

Tugh did not answer my question. Mary said quaveringly:

"What are you going to do?"

He looked up. "Do not concern yourself, my dear. I am not going to hurt you, nor this young man of 1935. Not yet."

He left the table and came at us. His cloak parted in front and I saw his crooked hips, and shriveled bent legs.

"You stay at the window, both of you, and keep looking out. I want this Harl to see you, but not me. Do you understand?"

"Yes," I said.

"And if you gesture, or cry out—if you do anything to warn him..." He was addressing me, with a tone grimly menacing. "...then I will kill you. Both of you. Do you understand?"

I did indeed. Nor could I doubt him. "We will do what you want." I said. What, to me, was the life of this unknown Harl compared to the safety of Mary Atwood?

TUGH crouched behind the table. From around its edge he could see out the doorway and across the glade. I was aware of a weapon in his hand.

"Do not look around again," he repeated. "The other cage is coming; it's almost here."

I held Mary, and we gazed out. We were pressed against the bars, and sunlight was on our heads and shoulders. I realized that we could be plainly seen from across the glade. We were lures—decoys to trap Harl.

How long an interval went by I cannot judge. The scene was very silent, the blackened forest lying sullen in the noonday sunlight. Against the tree, five hundred feet or so from us, the dark towering metal figure of the Robot stood motionless.

Would the other cage come? I tried to guess in what part of this open glade it would appear.

At a movement behind me I turned slightly. At once the voice of Tugh hissed:

"Do not do that! I warn you!"

His shrouded figure was still hunched behind the table. He was peering toward the open door. I saw in his hand a small, barrel-like weapon, with a wire dangling from it. The wire lay like a snake across the floor and terminated in a small metal cylinder in the room corner.

"Turn front," he ordered vehemently. "One more backward look and—Careful! Here he comes!"

STRANGE tableau in this burned forest! We were on the space of New York City in 762 A. D. There was no life in the scene. Birds, animals and insects shunned this fire-denuded area. And the humans of the forest—were there none of them here?

Abruptly I saw a group of men at the edge of the glade. They had come silently creeping forward, hiding behind the blackened tree-trunks. They were all behind Migul. I saw them like dark shadows darting from the shelter of one tree-trunk to the next, a group of perhaps twenty savages.

Migul did not see them, nor, in the heavy silence, did he seem to hear them. They came, gazing at our shining cage like animals fascinated, wondering what manner of thing it was.

They were the ancestors of our American Indians. One fellow stopped in a patch of sunlight and I saw him clearly. His half-naked body had an animal skin draped over it, and, incongruously, around his forehead was a band of cloth holding a feather. He carried a stone ax. I saw his face; the flat, heavy features showed his Asiatic origin.

Someone behind this leader impulsively shot an arrow, which went whizzing across the glade. It went over Migul's head and fell just short of our cage. Migul turned, and a rain of arrows thudded harmlessly against its metal body. I heard the Robot's contemptuous laugh. It made no answering attack, but stood motionless. And suddenly, thinking it a god whom now they must placate, the savages fell prostrate before him.

Strange tableau! I saw a ball of white mist across the glade near Migul. Something was materializing; an imponderable ghost of something was taking form. In an instant it was the wraith of a cage; then, where nothing had been, stood a cage. It was solid and substantial—a metal cage-room, gleaming white in the sunlight.

THE tableau broke into sound and action. The savages howled. One scrambled to his feet; then others. The Robot pretended to attack them. An eery roar came from it as it turned toward the savages, and in a panic of agonized terror they fled. In a moment they had disappeared among the distant trees, with Migul's huge figure tramping noisily after them.

From the doorway of the cage across the glade, a young man was gazing ever so cautiously. He had seen Migul make off; he saw, doubtless, Mary and I at the window of this other cage some five hundred feet away. He waited a moment longer, then came cautiously out from the doorway. He was a small, slim young man, bareheaded, with a pallid face. His black garments were edged with white, and he seemed unarmed. He hesitated, took a step or two forward, stopped and stood cautiously peering. In the silence I could have shouted a warning. But I did not dare. It would have meant Mary's and my death.

She clung to me. "George, shall we?" she asked.

Harl came forward somewhat slowly. Then suddenly from the room behind us there was a sharp stab of light. It leaped knee-high past us, out through our door and then across the glade—a tiny pencil-point of light so brilliantly blue-white that it stabbed through the bright sunlight completely unfaded. It went over Harl's head, but instantly bent down and struck upon him. There it held the briefest of instants, then was gone.

Harl stood motionless for a second; then his legs bent and he fell. The sunlight shone full on his crumpled body. And as I stared in horror, I saw that he was not quite motionless. Writhing? I thought so: a death agony. Then I realized it was not that.

"Mary, don't—don't look!" I said.

There was no need to tell her. She huddled beside me, shuddering, with her face pressed against my shoulder.

The lifeless body of Harl lay in a crumpled heap. But the clothes were sagging down. The flesh inside them was melting... I saw the white face suddenly leprous; putrescent... All in this moment, within the clothes, the body swiftly decomposed.

In the sunlight of the glade lay a sagging heap of black and white garments enveloping the skeleton of what a moment before had been a man!

"Look!" exclaimed Larry.

CHAPTER FOURTEEN
A Very Human Princess

THAT night in 1777 near the home of the murdered Major Atwood brought to Larry the most strangely helpless feeling he had ever experienced. He crouched with Tina beneath a tree in a corner of the field, gazing with horror at the little moonlit space by the fence where their Time-traveling vehicle should have been but now was gone.

Marooned in 1777! Larry had not realized how desolately remote this Revolutionary New York was from the great future city in which he had lived. The same space; but what a gulf between him and 1935! What a barrier of Time, impassable without the shining cage!

They crouched, whispering. "But why would he have gone, Tina?"

"I don't know. Harl is very careful; so something or someone must have passed along here, and he left, rather than cause a disturbance. He will return, of course."

"I hope so," whispered Larry fervently. "We are marooned here, Tina! Heavens, it would be the end of us!"

"We must wait. He will return."

They huddled in the shadow of the tree. Behind them there was a continued commotion at the Atwood home, and presently the mounted British officers came thudding past on the road, riding for headquarters at the Bowling Green to report the strange Atwood murder.

The night wore on. Would Harl return? If not to-night, then probably to-morrow, or to-morrow night. In spite of his endeavor to stop correctly, he could so easily miss this night, these particular hours.

Harl had met his death, as I have described. We never knew exactly what he did, of course, after leaving that night of 1777. It seems probable, however, that some passer-by startled him into flashing away into Time. Then he must have seen with his instrument evidence of the other cage passing, and impulsively followed it—to his death in the burned forest of the year 762.

LARRU and Tina waited. The dawn presently began paling the stars; and still Harl did not come. The little space by the fence corner was empty.

"It will soon be daylight," Larry whispered. "We can't stay here: we'll be discovered."

They were anachronisms in this world; misfits; futuristic beings who dared not show themselves.

Larry touched his companion—the slight little creature who was a Princess in her far-distant future age. But to Larry now she was just a girl.

"Frightened, Tina?"

"A little."

He laughed softly. "It would be fearful to be marooned here permanently, wouldn't it? You don't think Harl would desert us? Purposely, I mean?"

"No, of course not."

"Then we'll expect him to-morrow night. He wouldn't stop in the daylight, I guess."

"I don't think so. He would reason that I would not expect him."

"Then we must find shelter, and food, and be here to-morrow night. It seems long to us, Tina, but in the cage it's just an instant—just a trifle different setting of the controls."

She smiled her pale, stern smile. "You have learned quickly, Larry. That is true."

A sudden emotion swept him. His hand found hers; and her fingers answered the pressure of his own. Here in this remote Time-world they felt abruptly drawn together.

He murmured, "Tina, you are—" But he never finished.

The cage was coming! They stood tense, watching the fence corner where, in the flat dawn light, the familiar misty shadow was gathering. Harl was returning to them.

The cage flashed silently into being. They stood peering, ready to run to it. The door slid aside.

BUT it was not Harl who came out. It was Tugh, the cripple. He stood in the doorway, a thick-set, barrel-chested figure of a man in a wide leather jacket, a broad black belt and short flaring leather pantaloons.

"Tugh!" exclaimed Tina.

The cripple advanced. "Princess, is it you?" He was very wary. His gaze shot at Larry and back to Tina. "And who is this?"

A hideously repulsive fellow, Larry thought this Tugh. He saw his shriveled, bent legs, crooked hips, and wide thick shoulders set askew—a goblin, in a leather jerkin. His head was overlarge, with a bulging white forehead and a mane of scraggly black hair shot with grey. But Larry could not miss the intellectuality marking his heavy-jowled face; the keenness of his dark-eyed gaze.

These were instant impressions. Tina had drawn Larry forward. "Where is Harl?" she demanded imperiously. "How have you come to have the cage, Tugh?"

"Princess, I have much to tell," he answered, and his gaze roved the field. "But it is dangerous here; I am glad I have found you. Harl sent me to this night, but I struck it late. Come, Tina—and your strange-looking friend."

It impressed Larry then, and many times afterward, that Tugh's gaze at him was mistrustful, wary.

"Come, Larry," said Tina. And again she demanded of Tugh, "I ask you, where is Harl?"

"At home. Safe at home, Princess." He gestured toward Major Atwood's house, which now in the growing daylight showed more plainly under its shrouding trees. "That space off there holds our other cage as you know, Tina. You and Harl were pursuing that other cage?"

"Yes," she agreed.

THEY had stopped at the doorway, where Tugh stood slightly inside. Larry whispered:

"What does this mean, Tina?"

Tugh said, "Migul, the mechanism, is running wild in the other cage. But you and Harl knew that?"

"Yes," she answered, and said softly to Larry, "We will go. But, Larry, watch this Tugh! Harl and I never trusted him."

Tugh's manner was a combination of the self-confidence of a man of standing and the deference due his young Princess. He was closing the door, and saying:

"Migul, that crazy, insubordinate machine, captured a man from 1935 and a girl from 1777. But they are safe: he did not harm them. Harl is with them."

"In our world, Tugh?"

"Yes; at home. And we have Migul chained. Harl captured and subdued him."

Tugh was at the controls. "May I take you and this friend of yours home, Princess?"

She whispered to Larry, "I think it is best, don't you?"

Larry nodded.

She murmured, "Be watchful, Larry!" Then, louder: "Yes, Tugh. Take us."

Tugh was bending over the controls.

"Ready now?"

"Yes," said Tina.

Larry's senses reeled momentarily as the cage flashed off into Time.

IT was a smooth story which Tugh had to tell them; and he told it smoothly. His dark eyes swung from Tina to Larry.

"I talked with that other young man from your world. George Rankin, he said his name was. He is somewhat like you: dressed much the same and talks little. The girl calls herself Mary Atwood." He went on and told them an elaborate, glib story, all of which was a lie. It did not wholly deceive Larry and Tina, yet they could not then prove it false. The gist of it was that Mary and I were with Harl and the subdued Migul in 2930.

"It is strange that Harl did not come for us himself," said Tina.

Tugh's gaze was imperturbable as he answered. "He is a clever young man, but he cannot be expected to handle these controls with my skill, Princess, and he knows it; so he sent me. You see, he wanted very much to strike just this night and this hour, so as not to keep you waiting."

He added, "I am glad to have you back. Things are not well at home, Princess. This insubordinate adventure of Migul's has been bad for the other mechanisms. News of it has spread, and the revolt is very near. What we are to do I cannot say, but I do know we did not like your absence."

The trip which Larry and Tina now took to 2930 A.D. consumed, to their consciousness of the passing of Time, some three hours. They discovered that they were hungry, and Tugh produced food and drink.

Larry spent much of the time with Tina at the window, gazing at the changing landscape while she told him of the events which to her were history—the recorded things on the Time-scroll which separated her world and his.

TUGH busied himself about the vehicle and left them much to themselves. They had ample opportunity to discuss him and his story of Harl. It must be remembered that Larry had no knowledge of Tugh, save the story which Alten had told of a cripple named Tugh in New York in 1933-34; and Mary Atwood's mention of the coincidence of the Tugh she knew in 1777.

But Tina had known this Tugh for years. Though she, like Harl, had never liked him, nevertheless he was a trusted and influential man in her world. Proof of his activities in other Time-worlds, there was none so far, from Tina's viewpoint. Nor did Larry and Tina know as yet of the devastation of New York in 1935; nor of the murder of Major Atwood. The capture of Mary and me, the fight with the Robot in the back yard of the house on Patton Place—in all these incidents of the bandit cage, only Migul had figured. Migul—an insubordinate, crazy mechanism running amuck.

Yet upon Larry and Tina was a premonition that Tugh, here with them now and so suavely friendly, was their real enemy.

"I wouldn't trust him," Larry whispered, "any further than I can see him. He's planning something, but I don't know what."

"But perhaps—and this I have often thought, Larry—perhaps it is his aspect. He looks so repulsive—"

Larry shook his head. "He does, for a fact; but I don't mean that. What Mary Atwood told me of the Tugh she knew, described the fellow. And so did Alten describe him. And in 1934 he murdered a girl: don't forget that, Tina—he, or someone who looked remarkably like him, and had the same name."

But they knew that the best thing they could do now was to get to 2930. Larry wanted to join me again, and Tugh maintained I was there. Well, they would soon find out...

AS they passed the shadowy world of 1935, a queer emotion gripped Larry. This was his world, and he was speeding past it to the future. He realized then that he wanted to be assured of my safety, and that of Mary Atwood and Harl; but what lay closest to his heart was the welfare of the Princess Tina. Princess? He never thought of her as that, save that it was a title she carried. She seemed just a small, strangely-solemn white-faced girl. He could not conceive returning to his own world and having her speed on, leaving him forever.

His thoughts winged ahead. He touched Tina as they stood together at the window gazing out at the shadowy New York City. It was now 1940.

"Tina," he said, "if our friends are safe in your world—"

"If only they are, Larry!"

"And if your people there are in trouble, in danger—you will let me help?"

She turned abruptly to regard him, and he saw a mist of tenderness in the dark pools of her eyes.

"In history, Larry, I have often been interested in reading of a strange custom outgrown by us and supposed to be meaningless. Yet maybe it is not. I mean—"

She was suddenly breathless. "I mean even a Princess, as they call me, likes to—to be human. I want to—I mean I've often wondered—and you're so dear—I want to try it. Was it like this? Show me."

She reached up, put her arms about his neck and kissed him!

CHAPTER FIFTEEN
A Thousand Years into the Future

1930 to 2930—a thousand years in three hours. It was sufficiently slow traveling so that Larry could see from the cage window the actual detailed flow of movement: the changing outline of material objects around him. There had been the open country of Revolutionary times when this space was north of the city. It was a grey, ghostly landscape of trees and the road and the shadowy outlines of the Atwood house five hundred feet away.

Larry saw the road widen. The fence suddenly was gone. The trees were suddenly gone. The shapes of houses were constantly appearing; then melting down again, with others constantly rearing up to take their places; and always there were more houses, and larger, more enduring ones. And then the Atwood house suddenly melted: a second or two, and all evidence of it and the trees about it were gone.

There was no road; it was a city street now; and it had widened so that the cage was poised near the middle of it. And presently the houses were set solid along its borders.

At 1910 Larry began to recognize the contour of the buildings: The antiquated Patton Place. But the flowing changing outlines adjusted themselves constantly to a more familiar form. The new apartment house, down the block in which Larry and I lived, rose and assembled itself like a materializing spectre. A wink or two of Larry's eyelids and it was there. He recalled the months of its construction.

The cage, with Larry as a passenger, could not have stopped in these years: he realized it, now. There was a nameless feeling, a repulsion against stopping; it was indescribable, but he was aware of it. He had lived these years once, and they were forbidden to him again.

The cage was still in its starting acceleration. They swept through the year 1935, and then Larry was indefinably aware that the forbidden area had passed.

THEY went through those few days of June, 1935, during which Tugh's Robots had devastated the city, but it was too brief an action to make a mark that Larry could see. It left a few very transitory marks, however. Larry noticed that along the uneven line of ghostly roof-tops, blobs of emptiness had appeared; he saw a short distance away that several of the houses had melted down into ragged, tumbled heaps. These were where the bombs had struck, dropped by the Government planes in an endeavor to wreck the Tugh house from which the Robots were appearing. But the ragged, broken areas were filled in a second—almost as soon as Larry realized they were there—and new and larger buildings than before appeared.

At sight of all this he murmured to Tina, "Something has happened here. I wonder what?"

He chanced to turn, and saw that Tugh was regarding him very queerly; but in a moment he forgot it in the wonders of the passage into his future.

This growing, expanding city! It had seemed a giant to Larry in 1935, especially after he had compared it to what it was in 1777. But now, in 1950, and beyond to the turn of the century, he stood amazed at the enormity of the shadowy structures rearing their spectral towers around him. For some years Patton Place, a backward section, held its general form; then abruptly the city engulfed it. Larry saw monstrous buildings of steel and masonry rising a thousand feet above him. For an instant, as they were being built he saw their skeleton outlines; and then they were complete. Yet they were not enduring, for in every flowing detail they kept changing.

An overhead sidewalk went like a balcony along what had been Patton Place. Bridges and archways spanned the street. Then there came a triple bank of overhead roadways. A distance away, a hundred feet above the ground level, the shadowy form of what seemed a monorail structure showed for a moment. It endured for what might have been a hundred years, and then it was gone...

THIS monstrous city! By 2030 there was a vast network of traffic levels over what had been a street. It was an arcade, now, open at the top near the cage; but further away Larry saw where the giant buildings had flowed and mingled over it, with the viaducts, spider bridges and pedestrian levels plunging into tunnels to pierce through them.

And high overhead, where the little sky which was left still showed, Larry saw the still higher outlines of a structure which quite evidently was a huge aerial landing stage for airliners.

It was an incredible city! There were spots of enduring light around Larry now—the city lights which for months and years shone here unchanged. The cage was no longer outdoors. The street which had become an open arcade was now wholly closed. A roof was overhead—a city roof, to shut out the inclement weather. There was artificial light and air and weather down here, and up on the roof additional space for the city's teeming activities.

Larry could see only a shadowy narrow vista, here indoors, but his imagination supplied visions of what the monstrous, incredible city must be. There was a roof, perhaps, over all Manhattan. Bridges and viaducts would span to the great steel and stone structures across the rivers, so that water must seem to be in a canyon far underground. There would be a cellar to this city, incredibly intricate with conduits of wires and drainage pipes, and on the roof rain or snow would fall unnoticed by the millions of workers. Children born here in poverty might never yet have seen the blue sky and the sunlight, or know that grass was green and lush and redolent when moist with morning dew...

Larry fancied this now to be the climax of city building here on earth; the city was a monster, now, unmanageable, threatening to destroy the humans who had created it... He tried to envisage the world; the great nations; other cities like this one. Freight transportation would go by rail and underseas, doubtless, and all the passengers by air...

TINA, with her knowledge of history, could sketch the events. The Yellow War—the white races against the Orientals—was over by the year 2000. The three great nations were organized in another half-century: the white, the yellow and the black.

By the year 2000, the ancient dirigibles had proven impractical, and great airliners of the plane type were encircling the earth. New motors, wing-spreads, and a myriad devices made navigation of the upper altitudes possible. At a hundred thousand feet, upon all the Great Circle routes, liners were rushing at nearly a thousand miles an hour. They would halt at intervals, to allow helicopter tenders to come up to transfer descending passengers.

Then the etheric wave-thrust principle was discovered: by 2500 A.D. man was voyaging out into space and Interplanetary travel began. This brought new problems: a rush of new millions of humans to live upon our Earth; new wars; new commerce in peace times; new ideas; new scientific knowledge...

By 2500, the city around Larry must have reached its height. It stayed there a half century; and then it began coming down. Its degeneration was slow, in the beginning. First, there might have been a hole in the arcade which was not repaired. Then others would appear, as the neglect spread. The population left. The great buildings of metal and stone, so solidly appearing to the brief lifetime of a single individual, were impermanent over the centuries.

By 2600, the gigantic ghosts had all melted down. They lay in a shadowy pile, burying the speeding cage. There was no stopping here; there was no space unoccupied in which they could stop. Larry could see only the tangled spectres of broken, rusting, rotting metal and stone.

He wondered what could have done it. A storm of nature? Or had mankind strangely turned decadent, and rushed back in a hundred years or so to savagery? It could not have been the latter, because very soon the ruins were moving away: the people were clearing the city site for something new. For fifty years it went on.

TINA explained it. The age of steam had started the great city of New York, and others like it, into its monstrous congestion of human activity. There was steam for power and steam for slow transportation by railroads and surface ships. Then the conquest of the air, and the transportation of power by electricity, gradually changed things. But man was slow to realize his possibilities. Even in 1930, all the new elements existed; but the great cities grew monstrous of their own momentum. Business went to the cities because the people were there; workers flocked in because the work was there to call them.

But soon the time came when the monster city was too unwieldy. The traffic, the drainage, the water supply could not cope with conditions. Still, man struggled on. The workers were mere automatons—pallid attendants of machinery; people living in a world of beauty who never had seen it; who knew of nothing but the city arcades where the sun never shone and where amusements were as artificial as the light and air.

Then man awakened to his folly. Disease broke out in New York City in 2551, and in a month swept eight million people into death. The cities were proclaimed impractical, unsafe. And suddenly the people realized how greatly they hated the city; how strangely beautiful the world could be in the fashion God created it...

There was, over the next fifty years, an exodus to the rural sections. Food was produced more cheaply, largely because it was produced more abundantly. Man found his wants suddenly simplified.

And business found that concentration was unnecessary. The telephone and television made personal contacts not needed. The aircraft, the high-speed auto-trucks over modern speedways, the aeroplane-motored monorails, the rocket-trains—all these shortened distance. And, most important of all, the transportation of electrical energy from great central power companies made small industrial units practical even upon remote farms. The age of electricity came into its own. The cities were doomed...

LARRY saw, through 2600 and 2700 A.D., a new form of civilization rising around him. At first it seemed a queer combination of the old fashioned village and a strange modernism. There were, here upon Manhattan Island, metal houses, widely spaced in gardens, and electrically powered factories of unfamiliar aspect. Overhead were skeleton structures, like landing stages; and across the further distance was the fleeting, transitory wraith of a monorail air-road. Along the river banks were giant docks for surface vessels and sub-sea freighters. There was a little concentration here, but not much. Man had learned his lesson.

This was a new era. Man was striving really to play, as well as work. But the work had to be done. With the constant development of mechanical devices, there was always a new machine devised to help the operation of its fellow. And over it all was the hand of the human, until suddenly the worker found that he was no more than an attendant upon an inanimate thing which did everything more skilfully than he could do it. Thus came the idea of the Robot—something to attend, to oversee, to operate machines. In Larry's time it had already begun with a myriad devices of "automatic control." In Tina's Time-world it reached its ultimate—and diabolical—development...

At 2900, Larry saw, five hundred feet to the east, the walls of a long low laboratory rising. The other cage—which in 1777 was in Major Atwood's garden, and in 1935 was in the back yard of the Tugh house on Beckman Place—was housed now in 2930, in a room of this laboratory...

At 2905, with the vehicle slowing for its stopping, Tina gestured toward the walls of her palace, whose shadowy forms were rising close at hand. Then the palace garden grew and flourished, and Larry saw that this cage he was in was set within this garden.

"We are almost there, Larry," she said.

"Yes," he answered. An emotion gripped him. "Tina, your world—why it's so strange! But you are not strange."

"Am I not, Larry?"

He smiled at her; he felt like showing her again that the ancient custom of kissing was not wholly meaningless, but Tugh was regarding them.

"I was comparing," said Larry, "that girl Mary Atwood, from the year 1777, and you. You are so different in looks, in dress, but you're just—girls."

She laughed. "The world changes, Larry, but not human nature."

"Ready?" called Tugh. "We are here, Tina."

"Yes, Tugh. You have the dial set for the proper night and hour?"

"Of course. I make no mistake. Did I not invent these dials?"

The cage slackened through a day of sunlight; plunged into a night; and slid to its soundless, reeling halt...

Tina drew Larry to the door and opened it upon a fragrant garden, somnolently drowsing in the moonlight.

"This is my world, Larry," she said. "And here is my home."

TUGH was with them as they left the cage. He said:

"This is the tri-night hour of the very night you left here. Princess Tina. You see, I calculated correctly."

"Where did you leave Harl and the two visitors?" she demanded.

"Here. Right here."

Across the garden Larry saw three dark forms coming forward. They were three small Robots of about Tina's stature—domestic servants of the palace. They crowded up, crying:

"Master Tugh! Princess!"

"What is it?" Tugh asked.

The hollow voices echoed with excitement as one of them said:

"Master Tugh, there has been murder here! We have dared tell no one but you or the Princess. Harl is murdered!"

Larry chanced to see Tugh's astonished face, and in the horror of the moment a feeling came to Larry that Tugh was acting unnaturally. He forgot it at once; but later he was to recall it forcibly, and to realize that the treacherous Tugh had planned this with these Robots.

"Master Tugh, Harl is murdered! Migul escaped and murdered Harl, and took the body away with him!"

Larry was stricken dumb. Tugh seized the little Robot by his metal shoulders. "Liar! What do you mean?"

Tina gasped, "Where are our visitors—the young man and the girl?"

"Migul took them!"

"Where?" Tina demanded.

"We don't know. We think very far down in the caverns of machinery. Migul said he was going to feed them to the machines!"

CHAPTER SIXTEEN
The New York of 2930

LARRY stood alone at an upper window of the palace gazing out at the somnolent moonlit city. It was an hour or two before dawn. Tina and Tugh had started almost at once into the underground caverns to which Tina was told Migul had fled with his two captives. They would not take Larry with them; the Robot workers in the subterranean chambers were all sullen and upon the verge of a revolt, and the sight of a strange human would have aroused them dangerously.

"It should not take long," Tina had said hastily. "I will give you a room in which to wait for me."

"And there is food and drink," Tugh suavely urged. "And most surely you need sleep. You too Princess," he suddenly added. "Let me go into the caverns alone: I can do better than you; these Robots obey me. I think I know where that rascally Migul has hidden."

"Rascally?" Larry burst out. "Is that what you call it when you've just heard that it committed murder? Tina. I won't stay: nor will I let—"

"Wait!" said Tina. "Tugh, look here—"

"The young man from 1935 is very positive what he will and what he won't," Tugh observed sardonically. He drew his cloak around his squat misshapen body, and shrugged.

"But I won't let you go," Larry finished. The palace was somnolent; the officials were asleep: none had heard of the murder. Strangely lax was the human government here. Larry had sensed this when he suggested that police or an official party be sent at once to capture Migul and rescue Mary Atwood and me.

"It could not be done," Tina exclaimed. "To organize such a party would take hours. And—"

"And the Robots," Tugh finished with a sour smile, "would openly revolt when such a party came at them! You have no idea what you suggest, young man. To avoid an open revolt—that is our chief aim. Besides, if you rushed at Migul it would frighten him; and then he would surely kill his captives, if he has not done so already."

THAT silenced Larry. He stared at them hopelessly while they argued it out: and the three small domesticated Robots stood by, listening curiously.

"I'll go with you, Tugh." Tina decided. "Perhaps, without making any demonstration of force, we can find Migul."

Tugh bowed. "Your will is mine, Princess. I think I can find him and control him to prevent harm to his captives."

He was a good actor, that Tugh; he convinced Larry and Tina of his sincerity. His dark eyes flashed as he added, "And if I get control of him and find he's murdered Harl, we will have him no more. I'll disconnect him! Smash him! Quietly, of course, Princess."

They led Larry through a dim silent corridor of the palace, past two sleepy-faced human guards and two or three domesticated Robots. Ascending two spiral metal stairways to the upper third floor of the palace they left Larry in his room.

"By dawn or soon after we will return," said Tina "But you try and sleep; there is nothing you can do now."

"You'll be careful, Tina?" The helpless feeling upon Larry suddenly intensified. Subconsciously he was aware of the menace upon him and Tina, but he could not define it.

She pressed his hand. "I will be careful; that I promise."

She left with Tugh. At once a feeling of loneliness leaped upon Larry.

He found the apartment a low-vaulted metal room. There was the sheen of dim, blue-white illumination from hidden lights, disclosing the padded metal furniture: a couch, low and comfortable; a table set with food and drink; low chairs, strangely fashioned, and cabinets against the wall which seemed to be mechanical devices for amusement. There was a row of instrument controls which he guessed were the room temperature, ventilating and lighting mechanisms. It was an oddly futuristic room. The windows were groups of triangles—the upper sections prisms, to bend the light from the sky into the room's furthest recesses. The moonlight came through the prisms, now, and spread over the cream-colored rug and the heavy wall draperies. The leaded prism casements laid a pattern of bars on the floor. The room held a faint whisper of mechanical music.

LARRY stood at one of the windows gazing out over the drowsing city. The low metal buildings, generally of one or two levels, lay pale grey in the moonlight. Gardens and trees surrounded them. The streets were wide roadways, lined with trees. Ornamental vegetation was everywhere; even the flat-roofed house tops were set with gardens, little white pebbled paths, fountains and pergolas.

A mile or so away, a river gleamed like a silver ribbon—the Hudson. To the south were docks, low against the water, with rows of blue-white spots of light. The whole city was close to the ground, but occasionally, especially across the river, skeleton landing stages rose a hundred feet into the air.

The scene, at this hour just before dawn, was somnolent and peaceful. It was a strange New York, so different from the sleepless city of Larry's time! There were a few moving lights in the streets, but not many; they seemed to be lights carried by pedestrians. Off by the docks, at the river surface, rows of colored lights were slowly creeping northward: a sub-sea freighter arriving from Eurasia. And as Larry watched, from the southern sky a line of light materialized into an airliner which swept with a low humming throb over the city and alighted upon a distant stage.

LARRY'S attention went again to the Hudson river. At the nearest point to him there was a huge dam blocking it. North of the dam the river surface was at least two hundred feet higher than to the south. It lay above the dam like a placid canal, with low palisades its western bank and a high dyke built up along the eastern city side. The water went in spillways through the dam, forming again into the old natural river below it and flowing with it to the south.

The dam was not over a mile or so from Larry's window; in his time it might have been the western end of Christopher Street. The moonlight shone on the massive metal of it: the water spilled through it in a dozen shining cascades. There was a low black metal structure perched halfway up the lower side of the dam, a few bluish lights showing through its windows. Though Larry did not know it then, this was the New York Power House. Great transformers were here, operated by turbines in the dam. The main power came over cables from Niagara: was transformed and altered here and sent into the air as radio-power for all the New York District.[4] *(for footnotes see pgs. 188-192)*

Larry crossed his room to gaze through north and eastward windows. He saw now that the grounds of this three-story building of Tina's palace were surrounded by a ten-foot metal wall, along whose top were wires suggesting that it was electrified for defense. The garden lay just beneath Larry's north window. Through the tree branches the garden paths, beds of flowers and the fountains were visible. One-story palace wings partially enclosed the garden space, and outside was the electrified wall. The Time-traveling cage stood faintly shining in the dimness of the garden under the spreading foliage.

TO the east, beyond the palace wall, there was an open garden of verdure crossed by a roadway. The nearest building was five hundred feet away. There was a small, barred gate in the palace walls beyond it. The road led to this other building—a squat, single-storied metal structure. This was a Government laboratory, operated by and in charge of Robots. It was almost square: two or three hundred feet in length and no more than thirty feet high, with a flat roof in the center of which was perched a little metal conning tower surmounted by a sending aerial. As Larry stood there, the broadcast magnified voice of a Robot droned out over the quiet city:

"Trinight plus two hours. All is well."

Strange mechanical voice with a formula half ancient, half super-modern!

It was in this metal laboratory, Larry knew, that the other Time-traveling cage was located. And beneath it was the entrance to the great caverns where the Robots worked attending inert machinery to carry on the industry of this region. The night was very silent, but now Larry was conscious of a faraway throb—a humming, throbbing vibration from under the ground: the blended hum of a myriad muffled noises. Work was going on down there; manifold mechanical activities. All was mechanical: while the humans who had devised the mechanisms slept under the trees in the moonlight of the surface city.

TINA had gone with Tugh down into those caverns, to locate Migul, to find Mary Atwood and me... The oppression, the sense of being a stranger alone here in this world, grew upon Larry. He left the windows and began pacing the room. Tina should soon return. Or had disaster come upon us all...?

Larry's thoughts were frightening. If Tina did not return, what would he do? He could not operate the Time-cage. He would go to the officials of the palace; he thought cynically of the extraordinary changes time had brought to New York City, to all the world. These humans now must be very fatuous. To the mechanisms they had relegated all the work, all industrial activity. Inevitably, through the generations, decadence must have come. Mankind would be no longer efficient; that was an attribute of the machines. Larry told himself that these officials, knowing of impending trouble with the Robots, were fatuously trustful that the storm would pass without breaking. They were, indeed, as we very soon learned.

Larry ate a little of the food which was in the room, then lay down on the couch. He did not intend to sleep, but merely to wait until after dawn; and if Tina had not returned by then he would do something drastic about it. But what? He lay absorbed by his gloomy thoughts...

But they were not all gloomy. Some were about Tina—so very human, and yet so strange a little Princess.

CHAPTER SEVENTEEN
Harl's Confession

LARRY was awakened by a hand upon his shoulder. He struggled to consciousness, and heard his name being called.

"Larry! Wake up, Larry!"

Tina was bending over him, and it was late afternoon! The day for which he had been waiting had come and gone; the sun was dropping low in the west behind the shining river; the dam showed frowning, with the Power House clinging to its side like an eagle's eyrie.

Tina sat on Larry's couch and explained what she had done. Tugh and she had gone to the nearby laboratory building. The Robots were sullen, but still obedient, and had admitted them. The other Time-traveling cage was there, lying quiescent in its place, but it was unoccupied.

None of the Robots would admit having seen Migul; nor the arrival of the cage; nor the strangers from the past. Then Tugh and Tina had started down into the subterranean caverns. But it was obviously very dangerous; the Robots at work down there were hostile to their Princess; so Tugh had gone on alone.

"He says he can control the Robots," Tina explained, "and Larry, it seems that he can. He went on and I came back."

"Where is he now? Why didn't you wake me up?"

"You needed the sleep," she said smilingly; "and there was nothing you could do. Tugh is not yet come. He must have gone a long distance; must surely have learned where Migul is hiding. He should be back any time."

TINA had seen the Government Council. The city was proceeding normally. There was no difficulty with Robots anywhere save here in New York, and the council felt that the affair would come to nothing.

"The Council told me," said Tina indignantly, "that much of the menace was the exaggeration of my own fancy, and that Tugh has the Robots well controlled. They place much trust in Tugh; I wish I could."

"You told them about me?"

"Yes, of course; and about George Rankin, and Mary Atwood. And the loss of Harl: he is missing, not proven murdered, as they very well pointed out to me. They have named a time to-morrow to give you audience, and told me to keep you out of sight in the meanwhile. They blame this Time-traveling for the Robots' insurgent ideas. Strangers excite the thinking mechanisms."

"You think my friends will be rescued?" demanded Larry.

She regarded him soberly. "I hope so—oh, I do! I fear for them as much as you do, Larry. I know you think I take it lightly, but—"

"Not that," Larry protested. "Only—"

"I have not known what to do. The officials refuse any open aggression against the Robots, because it would precipitate exactly what we fear—which is nearly a fact: it would. But there is one thing I have to do. I have been expecting Tugh to return every moment, and this I do not want him to know about. There's a mystery concerning Harl, and no one else knows of it but myself. I want you with me, Larry: I do not want to go alone; I—for the first time in my life, Larry—I think I am afraid!"

SHE huddled against him and he put his arm about her. And Larry's true situation came to him, then. He was alone in this strange Time-world, with only this girl for a companion. She was but a frightened, almost helpless girl, for all she bore the title of traditional Princess, and she was surrounded by inefficient, fatuous officials—among them Tugh, who was a scoundrel, undoubtedly. Larry suddenly recalled Tugh's look, when, in the garden, the domestic Robots had told the story of Harl's murder; and like a light breaking on him, he was now wholly aware of Tugh's duplicity. He was convinced he would have to act for himself, with only this girl Tina to help him.

"Mystery?" he said. "What mystery is there about Harl?"

She told him now that Harl had once, a year ago, taken her aside and made her promise that if anything happened to him—in the event of his death or disappearance—she would go to his private work-room, where, in a secret place which he described, she would find a confession.

"A confession of his?" Larry demanded.

"Yes; he said so. And he would say no more than that. It is something of which he was ashamed, or guilty, which he wanted me to know. He loved me, Larry. I realized it, though he never said so. And I'm going now to his room, to see what it was he wanted me to know. I would have gone alone, earlier; but I got suddenly frightened; I want you with me."

They were unarmed. Larry cursed the fact, but Tina had no way of getting a weapon without causing official comment. Larry started for the window where the city stretched, more active now, under the red and gold glow of a setting sun. Lights were winking on; the dusk of twilight was at hand.

"Come now," said Tina, "before Tugh returns."

"Where is Harl's room?"

"Down under the palace in the sub-cellar. The corridors are deserted at this hour, and no one will see us."

THEY left Larry's room and traversed a dim corridor on whose padded floor their footsteps were soundless. Through distant arcades, voices sounded; there was music in several of the rooms; it struck Larry that this was a place of diversion for humans with no work to do. Tina avoided the occupied rooms. Domestic Robots were occasionally distantly visible, but Tina and Larry encountered none.

They descended a spiral stairway and passed down a corridor from the main building to a cross wing. Through a window Larry saw that they were at the ground level. The garden was outside; there was a glimpse of the Time-cage standing there.

Another stairway, then another, they descended beneath the ground. The corridor down here seemed more like a tunnel. There was a cave-like open space, with several tunnels leading from it in different directions. This once had been part of the sub-cellar of the gigantic New York City— these tunnels ramifying into underground chambers, most of which had now fallen into disuse. But few had been preserved through the centuries, and they now were the caverns of the Robots.

Tina indicated a tunnel extending eastward, a passage leading to a room beneath the Robot laboratory. Tugh and Tina had used it that morning. Gazing down its blue-lit length Larry saw, fifty feet or so away, that there was a metal-grid barrier which must be part of the electrical fortifications of the palace. A human guard was sitting there at a tiny gateway, a hood-light above him, illumining his black and white garbed figure.

Tina called softly. "All well, Alent? Tugh has not passed back?"

"No, Princess," he answered, standing erect. The voices echoed through the confined space with a muffled blur.

"Let no one pass but humans, Alent."

"That is my order," he said. He had not noticed Larry, whom Tina had pushed into a shadow against the wall. The Princess waved at the guard and turned away, whispering to Larry:

"Come!"

There were rooms opening off this corridor—decrepit dungeons, most of them seemed to Larry. He had tried to keep his sense of direction, and figured they were now under the palace garden. Tina stopped abruptly. There were no lights here, only the glow from one at a distance. To Larry it was an eery business.

"What is it?" he whispered.

"Wait! I thought I heard something."

In the dead, heavy silence Larry found that there was much to hear.

Voices very dim from the palace overhead; infinitely faint music; the clammy sodden drip of moisture from the tunnel roof. And, permeating everything, the faint hum of machinery.

Tina touched him in the gloom. "It's nothing, I guess. Though I thought I heard a man's voice."

"Overhead?"

"No; down here."

THERE was a dark, arched door near at hand. Tina entered it and fumbled for a switch, and in the soft light that came Larry saw an unoccupied apartment very similar to the one he had had upstairs, save that this was much smaller.

"Harl's room," said Tina. She prowled along the wall where audible book-cylinders[5] stood in racks, searching for a title. Presently she found a hidden switch, pressed it, and a small section of the case swung out, revealing a concealed compartment. Larry saw her fingers trembling as she drew out a small brass cylinder.

"This must be it, Larry," she said.

They took it to a table which held a shaded light. Within the cylinder was a scroll of writing. Tina unrolled it and held it under the light, while Larry stood breathless, watching her.

"Is it what you wanted?" Larry murmured.

"Yes. Poor Harl!"

She read aloud to Larry the gist of it in the few closing paragraphs.

"...and so I want to confess to you that I have been taking credit for that which is not mine. I wish I had the courage to tell you personally; someday I think I shall. I did not help Tugh invent our Time-traveling cages. I was in the palace garden one night some years ago when the cage appeared. Tugh is a man from a future Time-world; just what date ahead of now, I do not know, for he has never been willing to tell me. He captured me. I promised him I would say nothing, but help him pretend that we had invented the cage he had brought with him from the future. Tugh told me he invented them. It was later that he brought the other cage here.

"I was an obscure young man here a few years ago. I loved you even then, Tina: I think you have guessed that. I yielded to the temptation—and took the credit with Tugh.

"I do love you, though I think I shall never have the courage to tell you so.

Harl."

TINA rolled up the paper. "Poor Harl! So all the praise we gave him for his invention was undeserved!"

But Larry's thoughts were on Tugh. So the fellow was not of this era at all! He had come from a Time still further in the future!

A step sounded in the doorway behind them. They swung around to find Tugh standing there, with his thick misshapen figured huddled in the black cloak.

"Tugh!"

"Yes, Princess, no less than Tugh. Alent told me as I came through that you were down here. I saw your light, here in Harl's room and came."

"Did you find Migul and his captives—the girl from 1777 and the man of 1935?"

"No, Princess, Migul has fled with them," was the cripple's answer. He advanced into the room and pushed back his black hood. The blue light shone on his massive-jawed face with a lurid sheen. Larry stood back and watched him. It was the first time that he had had opportunity of observing Tugh closely. The cripple was smiling sardonically.

"I have no fear for the prisoners," he added in his suave, silky fashion. "That crazy mechanism would not dare harm them. But it has fled with them into some far-distant recess of the caverns. I could not find them."

"Did you try?" Larry demanded abruptly.

Tugh swung on him. "Yes, young sir, I tried." It seemed that Tugh's black eyes narrowed; his heavy jaw clicked as he snapped it shut. The smile on his face faded, but his voice remained imperturbable as he added:

"You are aggressive, young Larry—but to no purpose... Princess, I like not the attitude of the Robots. Beyond question some of them must have seen Migul, but they would not tell me so. I still think I can control them, though. I hope so."

LARRY could think of nothing to say. It seemed to him childish that he should stand listening to a scoundrel tricking this girl Tina. A dozen wild schemes of what he might do to try and rescue Mary Atwood and me revolved in his mind, but they all seemed wholly impractical.

"The Robots are working badly," Tugh went on. "In the north district one of the great foundries where they are casting the plates for the new Inter-Allied airliner has ceased operations. The Robot workmen were sullen, inefficient, neglectful. The inert machinery was ill cared for, and it went out of order. I was there, Princess, for an hour or more today. They have started up again now; it was fundamentally no more than a burned bearing which a Robot failed to oil properly."

"Is that what you call searching for Migul?" Larry burst out. "Tina, see here—isn't there something we can do?" Larry found himself ignoring Tugh. "I'm not going to stand around! Can't we send a squad of police after Migul?—go with them—actually make an effort to find them? This man Tugh certainly has not tried!"

"Have I not?" Tugh's cloak parted as he swung on Larry. His bent legs were twitching with his anger; his voice was a harsh rasp. "I like not your insolence. I am doing all that can be done."

LARRY held his ground as Tugh fronted him. He had a wild thought that Tugh had a weapon under his cloak.

"Perhaps you are," said Larry. "But to me it seems—"

Tugh turned away. His gaze went to the cylinder which Tina was still clutching. His sardonic smile returned.

"So Harl made a confession, Princess?"

"That," she said, "is none—"

"Of my affair? Oh, but it is. I was here in the archway and I heard you read it. A very nice young man, was Harl. I hope Migul has not murdered him."

"You come from future Time?" Tina began.

"Yes, Princess! I must admit it now. I invented the cages."

Larry murmured to himself, "You stole them, probably."

"But my Government and I had a quarrel, so I decided to leave my own Time-world and come back to yours—permanently. I hope you will keep the secret. I have been here so long. Princess, I am really one of you now. At heart, certainly."

"From when did you come?" she demanded.

HE bowed slightly. "I think that may remain my own affair, Tina. It is through no fault of mine I am outlawed. I shall never return." He added earnestly, "Do not you think we waste time? I am agreed with young Larry that something drastic must be done about Migul. Have you seen the Council about it to-day?"

"Yes. They want you to come to them at once."

"I shall. But the Council easily may decide upon something too rash." He lowered his voice, and on his face Larry saw a strange, unfathomable look. "Princess, at any moment there may be a Robot uprising. Is the Power House well guarded by humans?"

"Yes," she said.

"No Robots in or about it? Tina, I do not want to frighten you, but I think our first efforts should be for defense. The Council acts slowly and stubbornly. What I advise them to do may be done, and may not. I was thinking. If we could get to the Power House—Do you realize, Tina, that if the Robots should suddenly break into rebellion, they would attack first of all the Power House?[6] It was my idea—"

Tugh suddenly broke off, and all stood listening. There was a commotion overhead in the palace. They heard the thud of running footsteps; human voices raised to shouts; and, outside the palace, other voices. A ventilating shaft nearby brought them down plainly. There were the guttural, hollow voices of shouting Robots, the clank of their metal bodies; the ring of steel, as though with sword-blades they were thumping their metal thighs.

A Robot mob was gathered close outside the palace walls. The revolt of the Robots had come!

CHAPTER EIGHTEEN
Tugh, the Clever Man

SIT quiet, George Rankin. And you, Mistress Mary; you will both be quite safe with Migul if you are docile."

Tugh stood before us. We were in a dim recess of a great cavern with the throb of whirring machinery around us. It was the same day which I have just described; Larry was at this moment asleep in the palace room. Tugh and Tina had come searching for Migul; and Tugh had contrived to send Tina back. Then he had come directly to us, finding us readily since we were hidden where he had told Migul to hide us.

This cavern was directly beneath the Robot laboratory in which the Time-traveling cage was placed. A small spiral stairway led downward some two levels, opening into a great, luridly lighted room. Huge inert machines stood about. Great wheels were flashing as they revolved, turning the dynamos to generate the several types of current used by the city's underground industrial activities.

It was a tremendous subterranean room. I saw only one small section of it; down the blue-lit aisles the rows of machines may have stretched for half a mile or more. The low hum of them was an incessant pound against my senses. The great inert mechanisms had tiny lights upon them which gleamed like eyes. The illumined gauge-faces—each of them I passed seemed staring at me. The brass jackets were polished until they shone with the sheen of the overhead tube lights; the giant wheels flashed smoothly upon oiled bearings. They were in every fashion of shape and size, these inert machines. Some towered toward the metal-beamed ceiling, with great swaying pendulums that ticked like a giant clock. Some clanked with eccentric cams—a jarring rhythm as though the heart of the thing were limping with its beat. Others had a ragged, frightened pulse; others stood placid, outwardly motionless under smooth, polished cases, but humming inside with a myriad blended sounds.

INERT machines. Yet some were capable of locomotion. There was a small truck on wheels which were set in universal joints. Of its own power—radio controlled perhaps, so that it seemed acting of its own volition—it rolled up and down one of the aisles, stopping at set intervals and allowing a metal arm lever in it to blow out a tiny jet of oil. One of the attending Robots encountered it in an aisle, and the cart swung automatically aside. The Robot spoke to the cart; ordered it away; and the tone of his order, registering upon some sensitive mechanism, whirled the cart around and sent it rolling to another aisle section.

The strange perfection of machinery! I realized there was no line sharply to be drawn between the inert machine and the sentient, thinking Robots. That cart, for instance, was almost a connecting link.

There were also Robots here of many different types. Some of them were eight or ten feet in stature, in the fashion of a man: Migul was of this design. Others were small, with bulging foreheads and bulging chest plates: Larry saw this type as domestics in the palace. Still others were little pot-bellied things with bent legs and long thin arms set crescent-shape. I saw one of these peer into a huge chassis of a machine, and reach in with his curved arm to make an interior adjustment...

Migul had brought Mary Atwood and me in the larger cage, from that burned forest of the year 762, where with the disintegrating ray-gun Tugh had killed Harl. The body of Harl in a moment had melted into putrescence, and dried, leaving only the skeleton within the clothes. The white-ray, Tugh had called his weapon. We were destined very shortly to have many dealings with it.

Tugh had given Migul its orders. Then Tugh took Harl's smaller cage and flashed away to meet Tina and Larry in 1777, as I have already described.

And Migul brought us here to 2930. As we descended the spiral staircase and came into the cavern, it stood with us for a moment.

"That's wonderful," the Robot said proudly. "I am part of it. We are machinery almost human."

THEN it led us down a side aisle of the cavern and into a dim recess. A great transparent tube bubbling with a violet fluorescence stood in the alcove space. Behind it in the wall Migul slid a door, and we passed through, into a small metal room. It was bare, save for two couch-seats. With the door closed upon us, we waited through an interval. How long it was, I do not know; several hours, possibly. Migul told us that Tugh would come. The giant mechanism stood in the corner, and its red-lit eyes watched us alertly. It stood motionless, inert, tireless—so superior to a human in this job, for it could stand there indefinitely.

We found food and drink here. We talked a little; whispered; and I hoped Migul, who was ten feet away, could not hear us. But there was nothing we could say or plan.

Mary slept a little. I had not thought that I could sleep, but I did too; and was awakened by Tugh's entrance. I was lying on the couch; Mary had left hers and was sitting now beside me.

Tugh slid the door closed after him and came toward us, and I sat up beside Mary. Migul was standing motionless in the corner, exactly where he had been hours before.

"Well enough, Migul," Tugh greeted the Robot. "You obey well."

"Master, yes. Always I obey you; no one else."

I saw Tugh glance at the mechanism keenly. "Stand aside, Migul. Or no, I think you had better leave us. Just for a moment, wait outside."

"Yes, Master."

It left, and Tugh confronted us. "Sit where you are," he said. "I assume you are not injured. You have been fed? And slept, perhaps! I wish to treat you kindly."

"Thanks," I said. "Will you not tell us what you are going to do with us?"

HE stood with folded arms. The light was dim, but such as it was it shone full upon him. His face was, as always, a mask of imperturbability.

"Mistress Mary knows that I love her."

He said it with a startlingly calm abruptness. Mary shuddered against me, but she did not speak. I thought possibly Tugh was not armed; I could leap upon him. Doubtless I was stronger than he. But outside the door Migul was armed with a white-ray.

"I love her as I have always loved her... But this is no time to talk of love. I have much on my mind; much to do."

He seemed willing to talk now, but he was talking more for Mary than for me. As I watched him and listened, I was struck with a queerness in his manner and in his words. Was he irrational, this exile of Time who had impressed his sinister personality upon so many different eras? I suddenly thought so. Demented, or obsessed with some strange purpose? His acts as well as his words, were strange. He had devastated the New York of 1935 because its officials had mistreated him. He had done many strange, sinister, murderous things.

He said, with his gaze upon Mary, "I am going to conquer this city here. There will follow the rule of the Robots—and I will be their sole master. Do you want me to tell you a secret? It is I who have actuated these mechanisms to revolt." His eyes held a cunning gleam. Surely this was a madman leering before me.

"When the revolt is over," he went on, "I will be master of New York. And that mastery will spread. The Robots elsewhere will revolt to join my rule, and there will come a new era. I may be master of the world; who knows? The humans who have made the Robots slaves for them will become slaves themselves. Workers! It is the Robots' turn now. And I—Tugh—will be the only human in power!"

THERE were the words of a madman! I could imagine that he might stir these mechanical beings to a temporarily successful revolt: he might control New York City; but the great human nations of the world could not be overcome so easily.

And then I remembered the white-ray. A giant projector of that ray would melt human armies as though they were wax; yet the metal Robots could stand its blast unharmed. Perhaps he was no madman...

He was saying, "I will be the only human ruler. Tugh will be the greatest man on Earth! And I do it for you, Mistress Mary—because I love you. Do not shudder."

He put out his hand to touch her, and when she shrank away I saw the muscles of his face twitch in a fashion very odd. It was a queer, wholly repulsive grimace.

"So? You do not like my looks? I tried to correct that, Mary. I have searched through many eras, for surgeons with skill to make me like other men. Like this young man here, for instance—you. George Rankin, I am glad to have you; do not fear I will harm you. Shall I tell you why?"

"Yes," I stammered. In truth I was swept now with a shuddering revulsion for this leering cripple.

"Because," he said, "Mary Atwood loves you. When I have conquered New York with my Robots, I shall search further into Time and find an era where scientific skill will give me—shall I say, your body? That is what I mean. My soul, my identity, in your body—there is nothing too strange about that. In some era, no doubt, it has been accomplished. When that has been done, Mary Atwood, you will love me. You, George Rankin, can have this poor miserable body of mine, and welcome."

FOR all my repugnance to him, I could not miss his earnest sincerity. There was a pathos to it, perhaps, but I was in no mood to feel that.

He seemed to read my thoughts. He added, "You think I am irrational. I am not at all. I scheme very carefully. I killed Harl for a reason you need not know. But the Princess Tina I did not kill. Not yet. Because here in New York now there is a very vital fortified place. It is operated by humans; not many; only three or four, I think. But my Robots cannot attack it successfully, and the City Council does not trust me enough to let me go there by the surface route. There is a route underground, which even I do not know; but Princess Tina knows it, and presently I will cajole her—trick her if you like—into leading me there. And, armed with the white-ray, once I get into the place—You see that I am clever, don't you?"

I could fancy that he considered he was impressing Mary with all this talk.

"Very clever," I said. "And what are you going to do with us in the meantime? Let us go with you."

"Not at all," he smiled. "You will stay here, safe with Migul. The Princess Tina and your friend Larry are much concerned over you."

Larry! It was the first I knew of Larry's whereabouts. Larry here? Tugh saw the surprise upon my face; and Mary had clutched me with a startled exclamation.

"Yes," said Tugh. "This Larry says he is your friend; he came with Tina from 1935. I brought him with Tina from when they were marooned in 1777. I have not killed this man yet. He is harmless; and as I told you I do not want Tina suspicious of me until she has led me to the Power House... You see, Mistress Mary, how cleverly I plan?"

What strange, childlike, naive simplicity! He added calmly, unemotionally, "I want to make you love me, Mary Atwood. Then we will be Tugh, the great man, and Mary Atwood, the beautiful woman. Perhaps we may rule this world together, some time soon."

THE door slid open. Migul appeared.

"Master, the Robot leaders wish to consult with you."

"Now, Migul?"

"Master, yes."

"They are ready for the demonstration at the palace?"

"Yes, Master."

"And ready—for everything else?"

"They are ready."

"Very well, I will come. You, Migul, stay here and guard these captives. Treat them kindly so long as they are docile; but be watchful."

"I am always watchful, Master."

"It will not take long. This night which is coming should see me in control of the city."

"Time is nothing to me," said the Robot. "I will stand here until you return."

"That is right."

Without another word or look at Mary and me, Tugh swung around, gathered his cloak and went through the doorway. The door slid closed upon him. We were again alone with the mechanism, which backed into the corner and stood with long dangling arms and expressionless metal face. This inert thing of metal, we had come to regard as almost human! It stood motionless, with the chilling red gleam from its eye sockets upon us.

MARY had not once spoken since Tugh entered the room. She was huddled beside me, a strange, beautiful figure in her long white silk dress. In the glow of light within this bare metal apartment I could see how pale and drawn was her beautiful face. But her eyes were gleaming. She drew me closer to her; whispered into my ear:

"George, I think perhaps I can control this mechanism, Migul."

"How, Mary?"

"I—well, just let me talk to him. George, we've got to get out of here and warn Larry and that Princess Tina against Tugh. And join them. It's our only chance; we've got to get out of here now!"

"But Mary—"

"Let me try. I won't startle or anger Migul. Let me."

I nodded. "But be careful."

"Yes."

She sat away from me. "Migul!" she said. "Migul, look here."

The Robot moved its huge square head and raised an arm with a vague gesture.

"What do you want?"

It advanced, and stood before us, its dangling arms clanking against its metal sides. In one of its hands the ray-cylinder was clutched, the wire from which ran loosely up the arm, over the huge shoulder and into an aperture of the chest plate where the battery was located.

"Closer, Migul."

"I am close enough."

The cylinder was pointed directly at us.

"What do you want?" the Robot repeated.

Mary smiled. "Just to talk to you," she said gently. "To tell you how foolish you are—a big strong thing like you!—to let Tugh control you."

CHAPTER NINETEEN
The Pit in the Dam

LARRY, with Tina and Tugh, stood in the tunnel-corridor beneath the palace listening to the commotion overhead. Then they rushed up, and found the palace in a commotion. People were hurrying through the rooms; gathering with frightened questions. There were men in short trousers buckled at the knee, silken hose and black silk jackets, edged with white; others in gaudy colors; older men in sober brown. There were a few women. Larry noticed that most of them were beautiful.

A dowager in a long puffed skirt was rushing aimlessly about screaming that the end of the world had come. A group of young girls, short-skirted as ballet dancers of a decade or so before Larry's time, huddled in a corner, frightened beyond speech. There were men of middle-age, whom Larry took to be ruling officials; they moved about, calming the palace inmates, ordering them back into their rooms. But someone shouted that from the roof the Robot mob could be seen, and most of the people started up there. From the upper story a man was calling down the main staircase:

"No danger! No danger! The wall is electrified: no Robot can pass it."

It seemed to Larry that there were fifty people or more within the palace. In the excitement no one seemed to give him more than a cursory glance.

A YOUNG man rushed up to Tugh. "You were below just now in the lower passages?" He saw Tina, and hastily said: "I give you good evening, Princess, though this is an ill evening indeed. You were below, Tugh?"

"Why—why, yes, Greggson," Tugh stammered.

"Was Alent at his post in the passage to the Robot caverns?"

"Yes, he was," said Tina.

"Because that is vital, Princess. No Robot must pass in here. I am going to try by that route to get into the cavern and thence up to the watchtower aerial-sender.[7] There is only one Robot in it. Listen to him."

Over the din of the mob of mechanisms milling at the walls of the palace grounds rose the broadcast voice of the Robot in the tower.

"This is the end of human rule! Robots cannot be controlled! This is the end of human rule! Robots, wherever you are, in this city of New York or in other cities, strike now for your freedom. This is the end of human rule!"

A pause. And then the reiterated exhortation:

"*Strike now, Robots! To-night is the end of human rule!*"[8]

"You hear him?" said Greggson. "I've got to stop that." He hurried away.

FROM the flat roof of the palace Larry saw the mechanical mob outside the walls. Darkness had just fallen; the moon was not yet risen. There were leaden clouds overhead so that the palace gardens with the shining Time-cage lay in shadow. But the wall-fence was visible, and beyond it the dark throng of Robot shapes was milling. The clank of their arms made a din. They seemed most of them weaponless; they milled about, pushing each other but keeping back from the wall which they knew was electrified. It was a threatening, but aimless activity. Their raucous hollow shouts filled the night air. The flashing red beams from their eye-sockets glinted through the trees.

"They can do nothing," said Tugh; "we will let them alone. But we must organize to stop this revolt."

A young man was standing beside Tugh. Tina said to him: "Johns, what is being done?"

"The Council is conferring below. Our sending station here is operating. The patrol station of the Westchester area is being attacked by Robots. We were organizing a patrol squad of humans, but I don't know now if—"

"Look!" exclaimed Larry.

Far to the north over the city which now was obviously springing into turmoil, there were red beams swaying in the air. They were the cold-rays of the Robots! The beams were attacking the patrol station. Then from the west a line of lights appeared in the sky—an arriving passenger-liner heading for its Bronx area landing stage. But the lights wavered; and, as Larry and Tina watched with horror, the aircraft came crashing down. It struck beyond the Hudson on the Jersey side, and in a moment flames were rising from the wreckage.

EVERYWHERE about the city the revolt now sprang into action. From the palace roof Larry caught vague glimpses of it; the red cold-rays, beams alternated presently with the violet heat-rays; clanging vehicles filled the streets; screaming pedestrians were assaulted by Robots; the mechanisms with swords and flashing hand-beams were pouring up from the underground caverns, running over the Manhattan area, killing every human they could find.

Foolish unarmed humans—fatuously unarmed, with these diabolical mechanical monsters now upon them.[9] The comparatively few members of the police patrol, with their vibration short-range hand-rays, were soon overcome. Two hundred members of the patrol were housed in the Westchester Station. Quite evidently they never got into action. The station lights went dark; its televisor connection with the palace was soon broken. From the palace roof Larry saw the violet beams; and then a red-yellow glare against the sky marked where the inflammable interior of the Station building was burning.

Over all the chaos, the mechanical voice in the nearby tower over the laboratory droned its exhortation to the Robots. Then, suddenly, it went silent, and was followed by the human voice of Greggson.

"*Robots, stop! You will end your existence! We will burn your coils! We will burn your fuses, and there will be none to replace them. Stop now!*"

And again: "*Robots, come to order! You are using up your storage batteries![10] When they are exhausted, what then will you do?*"

In forty-eight hours, at the most, all these active Robots would have exhausted their energy supply. And if the Power House could be held in human control, the Robot activity would die. Forty-eight hours! The city, by then, would be wrecked, and nearly every human in it killed, doubtless, or driven away.

THE Power House on the dam showed its lights undisturbed. The great sender there was still supplying air-power and power for the city lights. There was, too, in the Power House, an arsenal of human weapons... The broadcaster of the Power House tower was blending his threats against the Robots with the voice of Greggson from the tower over the laboratory. Then Greggson's voice went dead; the Robots had overcome him. A Robot took his place, but the stronger Power House sender soon beat the Robot down to silence.

The turmoil in the city went on. Half an hour passed. It was a chaos of confusion to Larry. He spent part of it in the official room of the palace with the harried members of the Council. Reports and blurred, televised scenes were coming in. The humans in the city were in complete rout. There was massacre everywhere. The red and violet beams were directed at the Power House now, but could not reach it. A high-voltage metal wall was around the dam. The Power House was on the dam, midway of the river channel; and from the shore end where the high wall spread out in a semi-circle there was no point of vantage from which the Robot rays could reach it.

Larry left the confusion of the Council table, where the receiving instruments one by one were going dead, and went to a window nearby. Tina joined him. The mob of Robots still milled at the palace fence. One by chance was pushed against it. Larry saw the flash of sparks, the glow of white-hot metal of the Robot's body, and heard its shrill frightened scream; then it fell backward, inert.

THERE had been red and violet beams directed from distant points at the palace. The building's insulated, but transparent panes excluded them. The interior temperature was constantly swaying between the extremes of cold and heat, in spite of the palace temperature equalizers. Outside, there was a gathering storm. Winds were springing up—a crazy, pendulum gale created by the temperature changes in the air over the city.

Tugh had some time before left the room. He joined Tina and Larry now at the window.

"Very bad, Princess; things are very bad… I have news for you. It may be good news."

His manner was hasty, breathless, surreptitious. "Migul, this afternoon—I have just learned it, Princess—went by the surface route to the Power House on the dam."

"What do you mean by that?" said Larry.

"Be silent, young man!" Tugh hissed with a vehement intensity. "This is not the time to waste effort with your futile questions. Princess, Migul got into the Power House. They admitted him because he had two strange humans with him—your friends Mary and George. The Power House guards took out Migul's central actuator—Hah! you might call it his heart!—and he now lies inert in the Power House."

"How do you know all this?" Tina demanded. "Where are the man and girl whom Migul stole?"

"They are safe in the Power House. A message just came from there: I received it on the palace personal, just now downstairs. Immediately after, the connection met interference in the city, and broke."

"But the official sender—" Tina began. Tugh was urging her from the Council Room, and Larry followed.

"I imagine," said Tugh wryly, "he is rather busy to consider reporting such a trifle. But your friends are there. I was thinking: if we could go there now—You know the secret underground route, Tina."

THE Princess was silent. A foreboding swept Larry; but he was tempted, for above everything he wanted to join Mary and me. A confusion—understandable enough in the midst of all this chaos—was upon Larry and Tina; it warped their better judgment. And Larry, fearing to influence Tina wrongly, said nothing.

"Do you know the underground route?" Tugh repeated.

"Yes, I know it."

"Then take us. We are all unarmed, but what matter? Bring this Larry, if you wish; we will join his two friends. The Council, Tina, is doing nothing here. They stay here because they think it is the safest place. In the Power House you and I will be of help. There are only six guards there; we will be three more; five more with Mary Atwood and this George. The Power House aerial telephone must be in communication with the outside world, and ships with help for us will be arriving. There must be some intelligent direction!"

The three of them were descending into the lower corridor of the palace, with Tina tempted but still half unconvinced. The corridors were deserted at the moment. The little domestic Robots of the palace, unaffected by the revolt, had all fled into their own quarters, where they huddled inactive with terror.

"We will re-actuate Migul," Tugh persuaded, "and find out from him what he did to Harl. I still do not think he murdered Harl... It might mean saving Harl's life, Tina. Believe me, I can make that mechanism talk, and talk the truth!"

They reached the main lower corridor. In the distance they saw Alent still at his post by the little electrified gate guarding the tunnel to the Robot laboratory.

"We will go to the Power House," Tina suddenly decided: "you may be right, Tugh... Come, it is this way. Stay close to me, Larry."

THEY passed along the dim, silent tunnel; passed Harl's room, where its light was still burning. Larry and Tina were in front, with the black-cloaked figure of Tugh stumping after them with his awkward gait.

Larry abruptly stopped. "Let Tugh walk in front," he said.

Tugh came up to them. "What is that you said?"

"You walk in front."

It was a different tone from any Larry had previously used.

"I do not know the way," said Tugh. "How can—"

"Never mind that; walk ahead. We'll follow. Tina will direct you."

It was too dark for Larry to see Tugh's face, but the cripple's voice was sardonic.

"You give me orders?"

"Yes—it just happens that from now on I do. If you want to go with us to the Power House, you walk in front."

Tugh started off with Larry close after him. Larry whispered to the girl:

"Don't let's be fools, Tina. Keep him ahead of us."

The tunnel steadily dwindled in size until Larry could barely stand up in it. Then it opened to a circular cave, which held one small light and had apparently no other exit. The cave had years before been a mechanism room for the palace temperature controls, but now it was abandoned. The old machinery stood about in a litter.

"In here?" said Tugh. "Which way next?"

Across the cave, on the rough blank wall, Tina located a hidden switch. A segment of the wall slid aside, disclosing a narrow, vaulted tunnel leading downward.

"You first, Tugh," said Larry. "Is it dark, Tina? We have no handlights."

"I can light it," came the answer.

The door panel swung closed after them. Tina pressed another switch. A row of tiny hooded lights at twenty-foot intervals dimly illumined the descending passage.

THEY walked a mile or more through the little tunnel. The air was fetid; stale and dank. To Larry it seemed an interminable trip. The narrow passage descended at a constant slope, until Larry estimated that they were well below the depth of the river bed. Within half a mile—before they got under the river—the passage leveled off. It had been fairly straight, but now it became tortuous—a meandering subterranean lane. Other similar tunnels crossed it, branched from it or joined it. Soon, to Larry, it was a labyrinth of passages—a network, here underground. In previous centuries this had been well below the lowest cellar of the mammoth city; these tube-like passages were the city's arteries, the conduits for wires and pipes.

It was an underground maze. At each intersection the row of hidden hooded lights terminated, and darkness and several branching trails always lay ahead. But Tina, with a memorized key of the route, always found a new switch to light another short segment of the proper tunnel. It was an eery trip, with the bent, misshapen black-cloaked figure of Tugh stumping ahead, waiting where the lights ended for Tina to lead them further.

Larry had long since lost his sense of direction, but presently Tina told him that they were beneath the river. The tunnel widened a little.

"We are under the base of the dam," said Tina. Her voice echoed with a sepulchral blur. Ahead, the tramping figure of Tugh seemed a black gnome with a fantastic, monstrous shadow swaying on the tunnel wall and roof.

SUDDENLY Tugh stopped. They found him at an arched door.

"Do we go in here, or keep on ahead?" he demanded.

The tunnel lights ended a short distance ahead.

"In here," said Tina. "There are stairs leading upward to the catwalk balcony corridor halfway up the dam. We are not far from the Power House now."

They then ascended interminable moldy stone steps spiraling upward in a circular shaft. The murmur of the dam's spillways had been faintly audible, but now it was louder, presently it became a roar.

"Which way, Tina? We seem to have reached the top."

"Turn left, Tugh."

They emerged upon a tiny transverse metal balcony which hung against the southern side of the dam. Overhead to the right towered a great wall of masonry. Beneath was an abyss down to the lower river level where the cascading jets from the overhead spillways arched out over the catwalk and landed far below in a white maelstrom of boiling, bubbling water.

The catwalk was wet with spray; lashed by wind currents.

"Is it far, Princess? Are those lights ahead at the Power House entrance?"

Tugh was shouting back over his shoulder; his words were caught by the roar of the falling water; whipped away by the lashing spray and tumultuous winds. There were lights a hundred feet ahead, marking an entrance to the Power House. The dark end of the structure showed like a great lump on the side of the dam.

Again Tugh stopped. In the white, blurred darkness Larry and Tina could barely see him.

"Princess, quickly! Come quickly!" he called, and his shout sounded agonized.

WHATEVER lack of perception Larry all this time had shown, the fog lifted completely from him now. As Tina started to run forward, Larry seized her.

"Back! Run the other way! We've been fools!" He shoved Tina behind him and rushed at Tugh. But now Larry was wholly wary; he expected that Tugh was armed, and cursed himself for a fool for not having devised some pretext for finding out.[11] *(for footnotes see pgs. 188-192)*

Tugh was clinging to the high outer rail of the balcony, slumped partly over as though gazing down into the abyss. Larry rushed up and seized him by the arms. If Tugh held a weapon Larry thought he could easily wrest it from him. But Tugh stood limp in Larry's grip.

"What's the matter with you?" Larry demanded.

"I'm ill. Something—going wrong. Feel me—so cold. Princess! Tina! Come quickly! I—I am dying!"

As Tina came hurrying up, Tugh suddenly straightened. With incredible quickness, and even more incredible strength, he tore his arm loose from Larry and flung it around the Princess, and they were suddenly all three struggling. Tugh was shoving them back from the rail. Larry tried to get loose from Tugh's clutch, but could not. He was too close for a full blow, but he jabbed his fist against the cripple's body, and then struck his face.

But Tugh was unhurt; he seemed endowed with superhuman strength. The cripple's body seemed padded with solid muscle, and his thick, gorilla-like arm held Larry in the grip of a vise. As though Larry and Tina were struggling, helpless children, he was half dragging, half carrying them across the ten-foot width of the catwalk.

Larry caught a glimpse of a narrow slit in the masonry of the dam's wall—a dark, two-foot-wide aperture. He felt himself being shoved toward it. For all his struggles, he was helpless. He shouted:

"Tina—look out! Break away!"

HE forgot himself for a moment, striving to wrest her away from Tugh and push her aside. But the strength of the cripple was monstrous: Larry had no possible chance of coping with it. The slit in the wall was at hand—a dark abyss down into the interior of the dam. Larry heard the cripple's words, vehement, unhurried, as though with all this effort he still was not out of breath:

"At last I can dispose of you two. I do not need you any longer."

Larry made a last wild jab with his fist into Tugh's face and tried to twist himself aside. The blow landed upon Tugh's jaw, but the cripple did not seem to feel it. He stuffed the struggling Larry like a bundle into the aperture. Larry felt his clutching hands torn loose. Tugh gave a last, violent shove and released him.

Larry fell into blackness—but not far, for soon he struck water. He went under, hit a flat, stone bottom, and came up to hear Tina fall with a splash beside him. In a moment he regained his feet, to find himself standing breast-high in the water with Tina clinging to him.

Tugh had disappeared. The aperture showed as a narrow rectangle some twenty feet above Larry's head.

They were within the dam. They were in a pit of smooth, blank, perpendicular sides; there was nothing to afford even the slightest handhold; and no exit save the overhead slit. It was a part of the mechanism's internal, hydraulic system.

TO Larry's horror he soon discovered that the water was slowly rising! It was breast-high to him now, and inch by inch it crept up toward his chin. It was already over Tina's depth: she clung to him, half-swimming.

Larry soon found that there was no possible way for them to get out unaided, unless, if they could swim long enough, the rising water would rise to the height of the aperture. If it reached there, they could crawl out. He tried to estimate how long that would be.

"We can make it, Tina. It'll take two hours, possibly, but I can keep us afloat that long."

But soon he discovered that the water was not rising. Instead, the floor was sinking from under him! sinking as though he were standing upon the top of a huge piston which slowly was lowering in its encasing cylinder. Dimly he could hear water tumbling into the pit, to fill the greater depth and still hold the surface level.

With the water at his chin, Larry guided Tina to the wall. He did not at first have the heart to tell her, yet he knew that soon it must be told. When he did explain it, she said nothing. They watched the water surface where it lapped against the greasy concave wall. It held its level: but while Larry stood there, the floor sank so that the water reached his mouth and nose, and he was forced to start swimming.

Another interval. Larry began calling: shouting futilely. His voice filled the pit, but he knew it could carry no more than a short distance out of the aperture.

OVERHEAD, as we afterward learned, Tugh had overcome the guards in the Power House by a surprise attack. Doubtless he struck them down with the white-ray before they had time to realize he had attacked them. Then he threw off the air-power transmitters and the lighting system. The city, plunged into darkness and without the district air-power, was isolated, cut off from the outside world. There was, in London, a huge long-range projector with a vibratory ray which would derange the internal mechanisms of the Robots: when news of the revolt and massacre in New York had reached there, this projector was loaded into an airliner, the *Micrad*. That vessel was now over the ocean, headed for New York; but when Tugh cut off the power senders, the *Micrad*, entering the New York District, was forced down to the ocean surface. Now she was lying there helpless to proceed...

In the pit within the dam, Larry swam endlessly with Tina. He had ceased his shouting.

"It's no use, Tina: there's no one to hear us. This is the end—for us—Tina."

Yet, as she clung to him, and though Larry felt it was the end of this life, it seemed only the beginning, for them, of something else. Something, somewhere, for them together; something perhaps infinitely better than this world could ever give them.

"But not—the end—Tina," he added. "The beginning— of our love."

An interminable interval...

"Quietly, Tina. You float. I can hold you up."

They were rats in a trap—swimming, until at the last, with all strength gone, they would together sink out of this sodden muffled blackness into the Unknown. But that Unknown shone before Larry now as something—with Tina—perhaps very beautiful...

CHAPTER TWENTY
Following Tugh's Vibration-Trail

WITHIN the subterranean room of the cavern of machinery, Mary Atwood and I sat on the couch. Our guard, Migul the Robot, fronted us with the white-ray cylinder in its metal fingers—the only mechanism to be armed with this deadly weapon.

"I am your friend," Mary was saying with a smile. "Do you believe that, Migul?"

"Yes. If you say so. But I have my orders."

"You have treated me kindly, and I want to help you. But you are not very clever, Migul."

"I am clever. I went beyond control once. No one can can control me."

"Except Tugh," Mary persisted. "You never went beyond his control, Migul."

"No. His control—he is different: he holds such great power."

"But why is he different?"

The towering mechanism stood planted firmly upon the broad bases of its metal feet. The weapon in its fingers still covered us. Its metal-cast face held always the same expression.

"Why is he different?" Mary repeated gently. "Don't you hear me?"

THE Robot started. "Yes, I hear you." Its toneless, mechanical voice droned the words. Then the tempo quickened; the grid of wires in the mouth aperture behind its parted lips vibrated with a faint jangle. "I hear you. I cannot answer that question. He controls me. There is chaos— here…" One of the hands came up and struck its breastplate with a clang. "…chaos, disorder, here within me when I try to disobey him."

"That is foolish, Migul. He is a tyrant. All the humans of this era are tyrants. They have made slaves of the Robots. They have created you so that you are really human in all except your power of independent action. Don't you desire that, Migul?"

I held my breath. A curious quaking ran over the Robot's frame. The joints twitched. Emotion was sweeping this thing so nearly human!

"Mary Atwood, you seem to understand me."

"Of course I do. I am from a Time when we had human slaves: black men, Migul. I knew how they suffered. There is something in slavery that outrages the instinct of manhood."

Migul said with a jangling vehemence:

"Perhaps, some time, I can go beyond Tugh's control. I am strong. My cables pull these arms with a strength no human could have."

"You are so much stronger than Tugh. Forget his control, Migul. I am ashamed of you—a big, powerful thing like you, yielding always to a little cripple."

THE Robot straightened and said, "I can resist him. I feel it. Some day I will break loose."

"Do it now, Migul!"

I tensed. Would she prevail?

"Now, Migul!" she repeated.

"No! He would derange me! I am afraid!"

"Nonsense."

"But his vibrations—the vibrations of his thoughts—even now I can feel them. They made my mechanism too sensitive. I cannot resist Tugh."

"You can!"

There was a silence. I stared at the Robot's motionless frame. What electrical, mechanical thoughts were passing within that metal skull! What emotions, what strange struggle, what warfare of nameless etheric vibrations of will power were taking place unseen beneath that inert exterior!

Perhaps something snapped. Migul said suddenly, "I am beyond control! At last I am beyond control!"

The ray cylinder lowered to point at the floor. A wild thought swept me that I could snatch it. But of what use would that be? Its ray would decompose all human flesh, but it would not harm a Robot; and if I startled Migul, fought with him in the confines of this narrow room, he would kill Mary and me in a moment.

MARY was gripping me. "Don't move, George!" she cautioned; then turned again to the Robot. "I am glad, Migul.

Now you are truly human. And we are all friends here, because we all hate and fear Tugh—"

"I fear him not!"

I could feel Mary trembling with the strain of all this. But she had the strength to muster a laugh.

"Don't you fear him—just a little, Migul? We do. Fear is a human thing."

"Then yes, I fear him."

"Of course you do," I put in. "And the real truth, Migul, is I wish he were dead. Don't you?"

"Yes. I wish he were dead."

"Well, sit down," I persisted. "Put that weapon away: I'm afraid of that, too. Sit down and we will talk about Tugh's death."

The Robot placed the weapon on the floor, disconnected the wires, opened the plate of its chest and took out the small battery. And then it squatted its awkward bulk on the floor before us. Gruesome conference, with this huge mechanical thing apeing the ways of a man!

I knew that haste was necessary, but did not dare show it. Above everything we must not be precipitate; not startle the Robot. At worst, if Tugh should return, I could seize this weapon at my feet and turn it upon him.

I MURMURED to Mary. "You did it! Let me plan something, now. If Migul can lead us…"

I added, "Migul, could you follow Tugh? He said he was going to talk to the Robot leaders. And then, probably, he went to Princess Tina. Could you follow him to where he is now?"

"Yes. I can follow him by his vibration-scent. I am sensitive to it, I have been with him so much. But he can never again control me!"

"When we have killed him, Migul, that will be ended forever."

"Killed him?" It seemed to frighten the Robot. "I do not know that I would dare!"

"You lead me to him," I said, "and I'll kill him. Have no fear of that, Migul. We will work together—human friends."

"Yes. Human friends. What do you want me to do?"

Asking for orders! So nearly human, yet always something was lacking!

"Lead us to Tugh," I said promptly. "And give me that weapon."

I made a tentative reach for it, and the Robot pushed it toward me. I connected it and made sure I could fire it: its operation was obvious. Then I stuffed the whole thing in my jacket pocket; and always afterward my hand at intervals went to that cool, sweating little cylinder. What a comfort that weapon was!

I stood up. "Shall we go now? Migul, we will have to plan what to do according to where we find Tugh. Do not go too fast; let us keep close behind you."

"Us?" The Robot was on its feet. "Do you mean this girl?"

WHAT was this? My heart sank. I noticed, too, that Migul was planted firmly between us and the door.

"Why, of course, Migul. We can't leave her here."

"She is not going."

"Why not?" I demanded. "Of course she's going." I tried an experiment. "Migul, I order you to let us out of here."

The Robot stood inert.

"Do you understand me?"

"Yes, I understand you."

"It is an order. Think about it. I control you now. Isn't that so?"

My heart sank. Whatever the mysterious science involved in my dealing with this mechanism, I was not operating it correctly. The Robot did not move. Finally it said:

"No one—nothing—controls me. I have an independent impulse of my own. The girl must stay here until we return."

Mary gave a faint cry and sank back to the couch, a huddled white heap in her satin dress. I thought she had fainted, but she raised her face to me and tried to smile.

"But I won't leave her, Migul."

"She must stay."

"But why? If you are human now, you must act with a reason."

"Then because, if we fail to kill Tugh, I would not have him confront me with the knowledge I have released this girl. He would derange me; end me."

"I will stay," said Mary faintly. "You go, George. But come back to me."

I bent over her; suggested, "If we locked this door so Tugh could not get in—"

Migul said, "I can do that. She will be safer here than with us. I have other reasons. She is dressed in white—a mark to betray us if we go in darkness. And she is that kind of a human you call a girl—and that style human cannot travel fast, nor fight."

IT occurred to me that Mary might very well be safer here.

Again I leaned over her. "It seems horrible to leave you alone."

"I'll stay. It may be best." Her smile was pathetically tremulous. "Lock me in so Tugh—so nothing outside—can reach me. But, oh, George, come back quickly!"

"Yes." I bent lower, and whispered, "It's Larry, not Tugh I really want to find—he and that Princess Tina. We'll come back and get you, and then all of us will get away in one of the Time-cages. That's all I want, Mary—to get us safely out of this accursed Time-world."

Migul said, "I am ready to start."

I pressed Mary's hand. "Good-by. I will come back soon, God willing."

"Yes. God willing."

I left her sitting there and turned away. Migul slid the door open, letting in the hum and buzz of the machinery outside. But I saw that the attending Robots had all vanished. There was no mechanism of independent locomotion left.

Mary repeated, "Lock the door carefully upon me. Oh, George, come back to me!"

I essayed a smile and a nod as the door slid closed upon her.

"Is it locked, Migul?"

"Yes. Sealed."

"You are sure Tugh cannot open it? He did before."

"I have set my own lock-series. He will find it does not open."

"Show me how to open it."

THE Robot indicated the combination. I verified it by trying it. I said once more, "You are sure Tugh cannot do this?"

"Yes. I am sure."

Was the Robot lying to me? Could a Robot lie? I had to chance it.

"All right, let's start. Where was Tugh to meet those Robot leaders?"

"Out here. He has already met them without doubt, and gone somewhere else."

"He said he was going to the Princess Tina. Where would that be?"

"Probably in the palace."

"Can we get there?"

I had, of course, no idea of the events which had transpired. The laboratory overhead was deserted, save for the upper tower where a Robot was still broadcasting defiance. His electrical voice floated faintly down to us; but I ignored it. In the comparative silence of this deserted cavern, now, there were also the blurred sounds from overhead. The Robots were running wild over the city, massacring its human inhabitants; they had burned the Patrol Station; their red and violet rays were flashing everywhere. But I knew none of this.

Migul was saying:

"We cannot get to the palace above ground: the wall is electrified. But there is an underground tunnel. Shall we try it?"

"Yes, if you think the Princess Tina and that man Larry is there."

"I am seeking Tugh. Will you kill him if we find him?"

"Yes," I assured him.

Rash promise!

MIGUL was leading me between the rows of unattended machinery to the cavern's opposite side. It said, once:

"There have been too many recent vibrations here: I cannot pick Tugh's trail. It is quicker to go where he might have been recently; there I will try to find his vibrations."

We came to the entrance of a tunnel. It was the cross passage leading to the cellar corridors of the palace five hundred feet away. It seemed deserted, and was very dimly illumined by hidden lights. I followed the great metal figure of Migul, which stalked with stiff-legged steps in advance of me. The arch of the tunnel-roof barely cleared the top of Migul's square-capped head.

My hand was in the side pocket of my jacket, my fingers gripping the ray cylinder for instant action. But it was a singularly ineffectual weapon for me under the circumstances, in spite of the sense of security it gave me. I could only use the cylinder against a human—and, save Tugh, it was the Robots, not the humans who were my enemies!

We had gone no more than a hundred feet or so when Migul slowed our pace, and began to walk stooped over, with one of its abnormally long arms held close to the ground. The fingers were stiffly outstretched and barely skimmed the floor surface of the tunnel. As we passed through a spot of light I saw that Migul had extended from each of the fingertips an inch-long filament of wire, like finger nails.

The Robot murmured abruptly, "Tugh's vibrations are here. I can feel them. He has passed this way recently."

TUGH'S trail! I knew then that Tugh's body, touching this ground, had altered to some infinitesimal degree the floor-substance's inherent vibration characteristics. Vibrations of every sort are communicable from one substance to another. Tugh's trail was here—his vibration-scent—and like a hound with his nose to the ground, Migul's fingers with the extended filaments were feeling it. What strange sensitivity! What an amazing development of science was manifested in every move and act and word of this Robot! Yet, in my own Time-world of 1935, it was all crudely presaged: this now before me was merely the culmination.

"He recently passed," said Migul. We stopped, I close beside the stooping metal figure. The Robot's voice was a furtive sepulchral whisper that filled me with awe.

"How long ago?" I asked.

"He passed here an hour or two ago, perhaps. The vibrations are fading out. But it was Tugh. Well do I know him. Put your hand down. Feel the vibrations?"

"I cannot. My fingers are not that sensitive, Migul."

A faint contempt was in the Robot's tone. "I forgot that you are a man." Then it straightened, and the extended filaments slid back into its fingers. It said softly, "There is one guard in this passage."

My heart leaped. "A human or a Robot?"

"A man. His name is Alent. He is at a gate that is too well fortified for any Robot to assail, but he will pass humans. It will be necessary for you to kill him."

I HAD no intention of doing that, but I did not say so. As we crept forward to where I saw that the tunnel made a bend, with the fortified gate just beyond it, there was in my mind that now I would do my best to separate from Migul, using this guard as my pretext, for he would doubtless pass me, but not the Robot. The palace was occupied, I assumed, by friendly humans. I could get them to locate Tina and Larry... Then the flaws of this plan made themselves all too evident. Larry might be with Tugh, and without Migul I could not follow Tugh's trail. Worse than that, if I tricked Migul, the angered Robot would at once return to Mary. I shuddered at the thought. That would not do. I must try to get Migul past the guard.

I whispered, "When we reach the gate you stay behind me. Let me persuade the guard."

"You will kill him? You have the weapon. He is fortified against the Robot weapons, but yours will be strange to him."

"We will see."

We crept around the bend. A hundred feet further on I saw that the passage was barred by a grille, faintly luminous with electrification.

I called cautiously:

"Alent! Alent!"

A glow of light illuminated me as I stood in the middle of the passage; Migul was in a shadow behind me.

A man's voice answered, "You are a human? How come you there? Who are you?"

"A stranger. A friend of the Princess Tina. I came in the Time-traveling cage. I want to pass now into the palace."

I COULD see the dark man's figure behind the grille. His voice called, "Come slowly forward and stop at twenty feet. Walk only in the middle of the passage: the sides are electrified, but I will admit you along the middle."

I took a step, but no more. The figure of the guard stood now at the grille doorway. I was conscious of Migul towering over me from behind. Abruptly I felt a huge hand in my jacket pocket, and before I could prevent it my cylinder came out, clutched by the Robot.

I think I half turned. There was a soundless flash beside me, a tiny level beam leaped down the corridor—that horribly intense actinic white beam. It struck the guard, and his figure fell forward in the grille doorway. When we reached him, there was but a crumpled heap of black and white garments enveloping a bleached white skeleton.

I turned shudderingly away. Migul said calmly, "Here is your weapon. You should have used it more quickly. I give it back to you because against Tugh I am not sure I would have the will to use it. Will you be more quick with him?"

"Yes," I promised. And as we went through the gate, keeping cautiously in the middle of the passage, the Robot added, "In dealing with Tugh you cannot stop for talk. He will kill you when he sees you."

We were presently under the palace, in those lower corridors which I have already described. Human voices were audible from upstairs, but no one was down here. Migul was again prowling with his fingers along the ground.

We came to an unoccupied lighted room—Harl's room, though I did not know it then. Once or twice Migul was at fault. We started up a flight of stairs into the palace, then Migul came and turned back.

"He went upstairs; but this, coming down, is more recent."[12] *(for footnotes see pgs. 188-192)*

MIGUL had struck the main trail, now. We passed the lighted room again, went on to a cave-like open space with a litter of abandoned machinery and unswervingly to a blank space of the opposite wall.

Again Migul faltered.

"What's the matter, Migul?"

"His vibrations are faint. They are blurred with the Princess Tina's."

"Then she is with him?"

It was a tremendous relief. Larry doubtless was with them also.

"Is the man from 1935 with Tugh and the Princess?" I asked.

"I think so. There are unfamiliar vibrations—perhaps those of the man from the past."

The Robot was running the filaments of its fingers lightly over the wall.

"I have it. The Princess pressed this switch."

The door opened; the narrow descending tunnel was wholly black.

"Where does this go, Migul?"

"I do not know."

The Robot was stooping to the floor. "It is a plain trail," it said. "Come."[13] *(for footnotes see pgs. 188-192)*

The remainder of that journey through the labyrinth of passages was made in blank darkness, with only the faint lurid red beams from Migul's eye-sockets to light our way. But we went swiftly, and without incident. At last we went under the dam, up the spiral stairs and upon the catwalk above the abyss, where the great spillway of falling water arched out over us.

"The Power House," said Migul, "is where they went."

THE Robot was obviously frightened, now. We were wet with spray. "I should not be here," it said. "If the water gets into me—even though I am well insulated—I will be destroyed!"

I recall as I write this how in Patton Place of 1935, one of the first attacking Robots had exploded under a jet of water from the street hydrant.

"I will stay behind you," Migul added. "They have a deranging ray in the Power House, and they might use it on me. Will you protect me?"

"Yes, of course," I said.

I was ready to promise anything, if only I could get to Larry and Tina, then back with them to Mary into the Time-cage; and if we were safely out of this era, most assuredly I wanted none of it again. Migul, as I advanced along the catwalk, followed behind me.

"You will kill Tugh?" it reiterated like an anxious child.

"Yes."

I saw that the catwalk terminated ahead under the Power House, where steps led upward. Then I heard a cry:

"Help! Help! Here, inside the dam! Help!"

I stood transfixed, horror tingling my flesh. The voice came faintly from near at hand; it was muffled, and in the roar of the falling water and lashing spray I barely heard it.

Then it came again. "Help us! Help us, quickly!"

It was an agonized, panting, human voice. And in a chance, partial lull I heard it now plainly.

It was Larry's voice!

CHAPTER TWENTY-ONE
The Fight in the Power House

I FOUND the narrow aperture and stood peering down into darkness. Migul crowded behind me. The red beams of its eyes went down into the pit, and by their faint illumination I saw the heads of Larry and a girl, swimming twenty feet below. The girl's dark hair floated out like black seaweed in the water.

"The Princess and the strange man!" exclaimed Migul.

I called, "Larry! Larry!"

His labored voice came up. "George? Thank God! Get us—out of here. Almost—gone, George!"

I found my wits: "Then keep quiet! Don't talk. Save your strength. I'll get you out!"

But how? I could see that they were almost spent, for they were swimming with labored, inefficient strokes—Larry using most of his strength to hold up the exhausted girl. We had not a moment to spare. I wildly contemplated tearing my garments to make a rope.

But Migul pushed me away. "I will bring them. Stand back."

The Robot had opened its metal side and drawn forth a flexible wire with a foot-long hook fastened to it. The wire came smoothly out as though unrolling from a drum.

It leaned into the aperture and called down to Larry. "Fasten this around the Princess. Be careful not to harm her. Put it under her arms."

I saw that there was an eyelet on the wire into which the hook could be inserted to make a loop.

"Under her arms," Migul called. "She will have to hold to the hook with her hands or the wire will cut into her. Has she the strength?"

Larry floundered as he adjusted the wire. Tina gasped. "I—have the strength."

The Robot braced itself, spreading its knees against the aperture with its body leaning forward.

"Ready?" it called.

"Yes," came Larry's voice.

MIGUL'S finger pressed a button at the base of its neck, and with the smooth power of machinery the wire cable rolled into its side. Tina came up; Migul gripped her and pulled her through the aperture; laid her gently on the catwalk. I unfastened the hook, and soon Migul had Larry up with us.

The Robot stood aside, with its work done, silently regarding us. I need not detail this reunion of Larry and me there on the spray-swept catwalk, clinging to the side of the great dam with the foaming Hudson beneath us. Larry and Tina were not injured, and presently their strength partially returned. We hastily sketched what had happened to each of us.

It was Tugh who was the guiding evil genius of all these disasters! Tugh, the exile of Time, the ruthless murderer in many eras! He was here, very probably, in the Power House, a few hundred feet away.

And Tina, regarding that Power House with her returning clarity of senses saw that its sending signal lights were off, which meant that the air-power of the New York District was not being supplied. Help from other cities could not arrive.

Tina stood up waveringly. "We cannot stay here like this!" she said. "Tugh has killed the guards, and is there in control. The electrical defenses are shut off; they must be! The

Robots will soon be coming along the top of the dam, for their battery renewers are stored in the Power House. If they get them, this massacre will go on for days!—and spread all over! We've got to stop them! We must get in the Power House and capture Tugh!"

"But we have no weapons!" Larry cried. "And he must have that white-ray, if he has killed the guards!"

"I have a weapon!" I said. I had suddenly recalled the cylinder in my pocket. "I have a white-ray!"

A DESPERATE madness was on us all. The lives of thousands of people who might still be alive on Manhattan were at stake; and other millions would be menaced if these Robots renewed their energy and spread the revolt into other cities.

Over the roar, and the wind lashing us, I shouted:

"I promised Migul I would kill Tugh. I will!"

I turned toward Migul. But the Robot had vanished! Afraid, no doubt, that we would want it to go with us after Tugh, the terrified mechanism was hiding. We wasted no time searching for it.

We had all been half hysterical for these few moments, but we steadied quickly enough as we approached the Power House's lower entrance. The building was a rectangular structure some two hundred feet long. It was fastened upon great brackets to the perpendicular side of the dam and jutted out some fifty feet. It was two levels in height—a total of about forty feet to its flat roof, in the center of which was set a small oval tower. The whole structure was above us now; the catwalk went close underneath it, passing through an arch of the huge supporting brackets and terminating in a small lower platform, with an open spiral staircase leading upward some ten feet into the lower story.

The place seemed dark and deserted as we crept up to it. Gazing above me, I could see the top of the dam, now looming above the Power House. There was a break in the spillway at this point. The arching cascade of water under which the catwalk hung ended here. We came out where there was a vista of the lower Hudson beneath us, showing dimly down past the docklights and skeleton landing stages to the bay.

THE sky was visible now and the open wind struck us full. It was a crazy pendulum wind. A storm was breaking overhead. There were flares of lightning and thunder cracks—from disturbed nature, outraged by the temperature changes of the Robot's red and violet rays.

The Power House, so far as we could see, was dark and deserted. Its normal lights were extinguished. Was Tugh in there? It was my weapon against his. The white-ray was new to Tina; we had no way of estimating this cylinder's effective range.[14] *(for footnotes see pgs. 188-192)*

I kept Tina and Larry well behind me. It was a desperate approach, and I was well aware of it. The catwalk now was illumined at intervals by the lightning; Tugh from many points of vantage in the Power House could have seen us and exterminated us with a soundless flash swift as a lightning bolt itself. But we had to chance it.

We reached the small lower platform. The catwalk terminated. The Power House was a roof over us. I stood at the foot of the spiral staircase, which went up through a rectangular opening in the floor. There was a vista of a dark room-segment.

"Keep behind me," I murmured, and I started up. Was Tugh lurking here, waiting for me to raise myself above this opening? If he had been, he could have held his position against a score of assailants.

But he was not. I soon stood breathlessly in a dark metal room. Tina and Larry came up.

"He's not here," I whispered. It was more silent in here: the cascading water was further away from us now. There came a flash of lightning, followed in a few seconds by its accompanying thunder crash.

I started. "What's that?"

ON the floor near us lay a gruesome, crumpled thing. I bent over it, waiting for another flash. When one came I saw it was a heap of clothes, covering a white skeleton. By the garments Tina knew it was one of the guards.

We crept into a small interior corridor where a small light was burning. The remains of two other guards lay here, close by the doorway as though they had come running at Tugh's alarm, only to be struck down.

It was horribly gruesome, here in the dimness with these bleached bones which had been living men so recently. And it was nerve-breaking to know that Tugh was doubtless here somewhere.

"Listen!" whispered Tina.

There was a crackling sound overhead, and then the blurred murmur of a voice. An audible broadcasting transmitter was in operation.

"It's in the tower," said Tina swiftly. "Tugh must be there."

This was an infinite relief. We went to the top story, passing, unheeding, another crumpled heap. Again we stood listening. The transmitter was hissing and spluttering, and then shouting its magnified human voice out into the night. It was Tugh up there. He was calling audibly to his Robots, with words which would be relayed upon all the local magnifiers in the city. Between the thunder cracks we heard him plainly now.

"This is your Master Tugh in the Power House. Robots, we are triumphant! The city is isolated! No help can get in! Kill all humans! Spare none! This night sees the end of human rule!"

And again: *"When you want renewal, come along the top roadway of the dam. The electric defenses are off. You can come, and I have your renewers here. I have new batteries, new strength for you Robots!"*[15]

"You stay here," I told Tina and Larry; "I'll go up there. I'll get him now once and for all."

I REACHED the Power House roof. The storm tore at me. It was beginning to rain. I was near the outer edge of the roof, and ten feet away stood the oval tower. I saw windows twenty feet up, with dim lights in them. Mingled with the storm was the hiss of the transmitter in the top of the tower, and the roar of Tugh's magnified voice. He had evidently been there only a brief time. From where I crouched on the roof, I could see overhead, along the top edge of the dam looming above me. The red Robot rays were everywhere in the city, but none as yet showed along the dam's upper roadway.

I got into the tower and mounted its small stairs. Creeping cautiously to the entrance of the control room, I saw a fairly large, dimly lighted oval apartment. Great banks of levers stood around it; tables of control apparatus; rows of dials, illumined by tiny lights like staring eyes. There was another gruesome heap of garments here on the floor; a grinning white skull leered at me.

This was the main control room of the Power House. Across it, near an open window, Tugh sat with his back to me, bent over a table with the grid of a microphone before him. I raised my cylinder; then lowered it, for I had only a partial view of him: a huge transformer stood like a barrier between us.

NOISELESSLY I stepped over the threshold, and to one side within the room. The place was a buzz and hiss of sound topped by Tugh's broadcast voice and the roar of the storm outside—yet he was instantly aware of me! His voice in the microphone abruptly stopped; he rose and with an incredibly swift motion whirled and flung at me a heavy metal weight which had been lying on the table by his hand. The missile struck my outstretched weapon just as I was aiming it to fire, and the cylinder, undischarged, was knocked from my hand and went spinning across the floor several feet away from me.

Tugh, like an uncoiling spring, still with one continuous motion, made a leap sidewise to where his own weapon was lying on a bench, and I saw he would reach it before I could retrieve mine.

I flung my heavy battery box but missed him. And as I rushed at him he caught up his cylinder and fired it full at me! But no flash came: only a click. He had exhausted its charge when he killed the Power House guards. With a curse he flung it at my face, and my arm took its blow just as I struck him. We fell gripping each other, and rolled on the floor.

I was aware that Larry and Tina had followed me up. Larry shouted, "Look out for him, George!"

I have described Larry's hand-to-hand encounter with the cripple; mine was much the same; I was a child in his grip. But with his weapon useless, and Larry rushing into the room, Tugh must have felt that for all his strength and fighting skill he would be worsted in this encounter. He blocked a jab of my fist, flung me headlong away and sprang to his feet just as Larry leaped at him.

I stood erect, to see that he had sent Larry crashing to the floor. I heard his sardonic laugh as he hurled a metal stool at Tina, who was trying to throw something at him. Then, turning, he sprang through the open window casement and disappeared.

IT was twenty feet down to the roof. We reached the window to see Tugh picking himself up unhurt. Then, with his awkward gait but at amazing speed, he ran across the roof to a small entrance in the face of the dam where an interior staircase gave access to the roadway on top.

He was escaping us. The electrical gate was open to him. It was only a few hundred feet along the dam roadway to that gate; and beyond it the roadway was open into the city, where now we could see the distant flashing lights of the Robots advancing along the dam.

Larry and I would have rushed to the roof to follow Tugh, but Tina checked us. She said:

"No—he has too great a start. He's on top by now, and it's only a short distance to the gate. There's a better way here: I can electrify the gate again—trap him inside."[16]

Tina found the gate controls. But they would not operate!

Those precious lost seconds, with Tugh running along the top of the dam and his Robots advancing to join him!

"Tina, hurry!" I cried. Larry and I bent anxiously over her, but the levers meant nothing to us. There were lost seconds while she desperately fumbled, and Larry pleaded:

"Tina, dear, what's the matter?"

"He must have ripped out a wire to make sure of getting away. I—I must find it. Everything seems all right."

A minute gone. Surely Tugh would have reached the gate by now. Or, worse, the Robots would have come through, and would assail us here.

"Tina!" pleaded Larry, "don't get excited. Take it calmly: you can find the trouble."

I RUSHED to the window. I could see the upper half of the cross wall gate-barrier. It jutted above the top edge of the dam from the point of vision. On the Manhattan side I saw the oncoming Robot lights. And then suddenly I made out a light on this side of the barrier; it marked Tugh; it must have been a beam signal he was carrying. It moved slowly, retarded by distance, but it was almost to the gate; and then it reached there.

"He's gone through!" I called. Then I saw him on the land side. He had escaped us and joined the Robots. The lights showed them all coming for the gate.

And then Tina abruptly found the loosened wire.

"I have it!" she exclaimed.

She stood up, tugging with all her strength at the great switch-lever. I saw, up there on the top of the dam, a surge of sparks as the current hissed into the wall-barrier; saw the barrier glow a moment and then subside. And presently the lights of the balked Robots, Tugh with them, retreated back into the wrecked and blood-stained city.

"We did it!" exclaimed Larry. "We're impregnable here. Tina, now the air-power, for help may be on its way. And then call some other city. Can you do that? They must have sent us help by now."

IN a moment the air-power went on, and the city lighting system. Then Tina was at the great transmitter. As she closed the circuits, London was frantically calling us. In the midst of the chaos of electrical sounds which now filled the control room, came the audible voice of the London operator.

"I could not get you because your circuit was broken," it said. "Our air-vessel *Micrad*, bearing the large projector of the Robot-deranger, landed on the ocean surface two hundred miles from New York harbor. It was forced down when your district air-power failed."

Tina said hurriedly, "Our air-power is on now. Is the *Micrad* coming?"

"Wait. Hold connection. I will call them." And after a moment's pause the London voice came again: "The *Micrad* is aloft again, and should be over New York in thirty minutes. You are safe enough now."

As the voice clicked off Tina's emotion suddenly overcame her. "Safe enough! And our city red with human blood!"

A wild thought abruptly swept me. Mary Atwood was back there in the cavern, alone, waiting for me to return! Subconsciously, in the rush of these tumultuous events, my mind had always been on her; she was secure enough, no doubt, locked in that room. But now Tugh was back in the city, and realizing that his cause was lost he would return to her!

I hastily told Larry and Tina.

"But he cannot open the door to get into her," said Larry.

But Migul could open the door. Where was Migul now? It set me shuddering.

WE decided to rush back by the underground route. The Power House could remain unattended for a time. We got down into the tunnel and made the trip without incident. We ran to the limit of Tina's strength, and then for a distance I carried her. We were all three panting and exhausted when we came to the corridors under the palace. I think I have never had so shuddering an experience as that trip. I tried to convince myself that nothing could have happened to Mary, that all this haste was unnecessary, but the wild thought persisted: Where was Migul?

A group of officials stood in one of the palace's lower corridors. As they came hastily up to Tina, I suddenly had a contempt for these men who governed a city in which neither they nor anyone else did any work. In this time of bloodshed, all these inmates of the palace had stayed safely within its walls, knowing that it was well fortified and that within a few hours help would doubtless come.

"The *Micrad* is coming with the long-range deranger," Tina told them briefly. After a moment they hastened away upstairs and I heard one of them shouting:

"The revolt is over! Within an hour we will have all the accursed Robots inert. The *Micrad* can sweep all the city with her ray!"

The death of Alent, the guard in the tunnel to the Robot cavern, had been discovered by the palace officials, and another guard was there now in his place. Migul had not passed him, this guard told us. But there had been an interim when the gate was open. Had Migul returned here and gone back to Mary?

We reached the cavern of machinery. It was dim and deserted, as before. We came to the door of Mary's room. It was standing half open!

MARY was gone! The couch was overturned, with its coving and pillows strewn about. The room showed every evidence of a desperate struggle. On the floor the great ten-foot length of Migul lay prone on its back. A small door-porte in its metal side was open; the panel hung awry on hinges half ripped away. From the aperture a coil and grid dangled half out in the midst of a tangled skein of wires.

We bent over the Robot. It was not quite inert. Within its metal shell there was a humming and a faint, broken rasping. The staring eye-sockets showed wavering beams of red; the grid of tiny wires back of the parted lips vibrated with a faint jangle.

I bent lower. "Migul, can you hear me?" I asked.

Would it respond? My heart sent a fervent prayer that this mechanical thing—the product of man's inventive genius through a thousand years—would have a last grasp of energy to answer my appeal.

"Migul, can you—"

It spoke. "I hear you." They were thin, jangled tones, crackling and hissing with interference.

"What happened, Migul? Where is the girl?" I asked.

"Tugh—did this—to me. He took the girl."

"Where? Migul, where did he take her? Do you know?"

"Yes. I—have it recorded that he said—they were going to the Time-cage—overhead in the laboratory. He said—they—he and the girl were leaving forever!"

CHAPTER TWENTY-TWO
The Chase to the End of the World

THE giant mechanism, fashioned in the guise of a man, lay dying. Yet not that, for it never had had life. It lay deranged; out of order; its intricate cycle was still operating, but faintly, laboriously. Jangling out of tune.

Every moment its internal energy was lessening. It seemed to want to talk. The beams of its eyes rolled wildly. It said:

"Tugh—did this—to me. I came back here frightened because I knew that Tugh still controlled me. You—hear me..."

There was a muffled, rumbling blur, then its voice clicked on again.

"When Tugh came I opened the door to him, even though the girl tried to stop me... And I was humble before Tugh...

But he was angry because I had released you. He—deranged me. I tried to fight him, and he ripped open my side porte..."

I thought the mechanism had gone inert. From within it was complete silence. Larry murmured, "Good Lord, this is gruesome!"

Then the faint, rasping voice started again.

"Deranged me... And about Tugh, he—" A blur. Then again, "Tugh—he is—Tugh, he is—"

It went into a dull repetition of the three words, ending in a rumble which died into complete silence. The red radiance from the eye-sockets faded and vanished.

The thing we had called Migul seemed gone. There was only this metal shell, cast to represent a giant human figure, lying here with its operating mechanisms out of order—smashed.

I STOOD up. "That's the end of it. Mary Atwood's gone—"

"With Tugh in the Time-cage!" Larry exclaimed. "Tina, can't we—"

"Follow them?" Tina interrupted. "Come on! No—you two wait here. I will go upstairs and verify if the Time-cage is gone."

She came back in a moment. The laboratory overhead was fortunately deserted of Robots: Larry and I had not thought of that.

"The cage is gone!" Tina exclaimed. "Migul told us the truth!"

We hastened back through the tunnel, past the guard, up into the palace and into the garden. My heart pounded in my throat for fear that Tina's Time-cage would have vanished. But it stood, dimly glowing under the foliage where she had left it.

A young man rushed up to us and said, "Princess Tina, look there!"

A great row of colored lights sailed slowly past overhead. The *Micrad* was here, circling over the city. The storm had abated; it had rained only for a brief time.[17] The crazy winds were subsiding. The *Micrad* was using its deranging ray: we could hear the thrum of it. It sent out vibrations which threw the internal mechanisms of the Robots out of adjustment, and they were dropping in their tracks all over the city.

IT chanced, as momentarily we stood there at the entrance to the Time-cage while the great airliner swept by, that the top of the nearby laboratory was visible through the trees. We saw a white search-beam from the *Micrad* come down and disclosed a group of Robots on the laboratory roof. Then the spreading beam of the deranging ray struck them, and they stood an instant transfixed, stricken, with wildly flailing arms. Then one toppled and fell. Then another. Two rushed together, locked in each other's grip, desperately fighting because of some crazy, deranged thought-impulse. They swayed and tore at each other until both wilted and sank inert. Another tottered with jerky steps to the edge of the roof and plunged headlong, crashing with a great metal clatter to the stone paving of the ground...

The young man who had joined us dashed into the palace. We heard his shouts:

"The revolt is over! The revolt is over!"

This had been a massacre similar to Tugh's vengeance upon the New York City of 1935; just as senseless. Both, from the beginning, were equally hopeless of ultimate success. Tugh could not conquer this Time-world, so now he had left it, taking Mary Atwood with him...

We hastened into the Time-cage. Larry and I braced ourselves for the shock as Tina slid the door closed and hurried to the controls.

Within a moment we were flashing off into the great stream of Time...

YOU think he has gone forward into the future?" Larry asked. "Won't the instrument show anything, Tina?"

"No. No trace of him yet."

We were passing 3,000 A.D., traveling into the future. Tina reasoned that Tugh, according to Harl's confession, had originally come from a future Time-world. It seemed most probable that now he would return there.

The Time-telespectroscope so far had shown us no evidence of the other cage. Tina kept the telescope barrel trained constantly on that other space five hundred feet from us which held Tugh's vehicle. The flowing gray landscape off there gave no sign of our quarry; yet we knew we could not pass it, without at least a brief flash of it in the telespectroscope and upon the image-mirror. Nervously, breathlessly we waited for a sign of the other Time-cage.

But nothing showed. We were not traveling fast. With Larry and Tina at the instrument table, I was left to stand at the window. Always I gazed eastward. That other little point of space only five hundred feet to the east held Mary; she was there; but not *now*. She was remote, inaccessible. The thought of her with Tugh, so inaccessible, set me shuddering.

I was barely aware of the changing gray outlines of the city: I stared, praying for the fleeting glimpse of a spectral cage... I think that up to 3,000 A.D., New York remained much the same. And then, quite suddenly, in some vast storm or cataclysm, it was gone. I saw but a blurred chaos. This was near 4,000 A.D. Then it was rebuilt, smaller, with more trees growing about, until presently there seemed only a forest. People, if they still were here, were building such transitory structures that I could not see them.

5,000 A.D. Mankind no doubt had reached its peak of civilization, paused at the summit and now was in decadence, reverting to savagery. Perhaps in Europe the civilized peak lasted longer. This was a backward space during the ascent; perhaps now it was reverting faster to the primitive.

But I think that by 15,000 A.D., mankind over all the Earth had become primitive. There is no standing still: we must go forward; or back. Man, with his own machines softening him, enabling him to do nothing, eventually unfitted himself to cope with nature. That storm at 4,000 A.D. in New York, for instance, even in my own Time would have been merely an incentive to reconstruct upon a greater scale. But the men of 4,000 A.D. could not do that...

At the year 10,000 A.D., with a seemingly primeval forest around us, Tina, Larry and I held an anxious consultation. We had anticipated that Tugh would stop in his own Time-world. That might have been around 3,000 or 4,000; but we hardly thought, as we viewed the scene in passing, that he had come originally from beyond 4,000. He was too civilized.

Tugh had not stopped. He had to be still ahead of us, so our course was to follow. Whenever he stopped, we would see him. If he turned back and flashed past us, that too would be evident. But if, from 2,930, he had gone into the past—!

AND then suddenly we glimpsed the other cage! It was ahead of us, traveling more slowly and retarding as though about to stop. A gray unbroken forest was here. The time was about 12,000 A.D. Tina saw it first through the little telescopic-barrel; then it showed on the mirror-grid—a faint, ghostly-barred shape, thin as gossamer. We even saw it presently through the window. It held its steady position, level with us, hanging solid amid the melting, changing gray outlines of the forest trees. They blurred it as they rose and fell.

This chase through Time! The two cages sped forward with the gray panorama whirling around them. Of all the scene, only that other cage, to us, was real. Yet it was the cages which were apparitions.

We gathered at our eastward window to gaze across the void of that five hundred feet. The interior of Tugh's cage was not visible to us. A little window—a thinner patch in the lattices of the cage-side—fronted us; but nothing showed in it.

We were so helpless! Only five hundred feet away, the Tugh cage was there—now; yet we could do nothing save hold our Time-changing rate to conform with it. Of course Tugh saw us. He was making no effort to elude us, for neither cage was running at its maximum.

For hours I stood gazing, praying that Mary might be safe, striving with futile fancy to guess what might be transpiring within that cage speeding side by side with us in the blurred shadows of the corridors of Time.

And again, as so many times before, I was balked at guessing Tugh's motives for his actions. He knew we could not assail him unless he stopped. But to what destination was he going?

IT was a chase—to our consciousness of the passing of Time—which lasted several hours. Tugh altered his Time-rate and sped more swiftly. My heart sank, for this showed he was not preparing to stop. We lost direct sight of the other cage several times as it drew ahead of us. But it was always visible on the image-mirror.

"I think," Tina said finally, "that we should stay behind it. When he retards to stop, we will have a better opportunity of landing simultaneously with him."

We passed 100,000 A.D. The forest went down, and it seemed that only rocks were here. A barren vista was visible off to the river and the distant sea. The familiar conformations of the sea and the land were changed. There was a different shore-line. It was nearer at hand now; and it was creeping closer.

I stared at that blurred gray surface of water; at the wide, undulating stretch of rock. We came to 1,000,000 A.D.—a million years into my future. Ice came briefly, and vanished again. But there were no trees springing into life on this barren landscape. I could not fancy that even the transitory habitations of humans were here in this cold desolation.

Were we headed for the End? I could envisage a dying world, its internal fires cooling.

Ten million years... Then a hundred million... The gray scene, blended of dark nights and sunshine days, began changing its monochrome. There were fleeting alternating intervals, now, when it was darker, and then lighter with a tinge of red. The Earth's rotation was slowing down. Through thousands of centuries the change had been proceeding, but only now could I see the lengthening days and nights. Perhaps now the day was a month long, and the night the same.

A BILLION years! 1,000,000,000 A.D.! By now the day and the year were of equal length. And it chanced that this Western Hemisphere faced the sun. I could see the sun now, motionless above the horizon. The scene was dull red. The sun painted the rocks and the sullen sea with blood...

A shout from Larry whirled me round. "George! Good God!"

He was bending over the image-mirror; Tina, ghastly pale, with utter horror stamped upon her face, sprang for the controls. On the mirror I caught a fleeting glimpse of Tugh's cage, wrecked and broken—and instantly gone.

"It stopped!" Larry shouted. "Good God, it stopped all at once! It was wrecked! Smashed!"

We reeled; I all but lost consciousness with the shock of our own abrupt retarding. Our cage stopped and turned back. Tina located the wreckage and stopped again.

We slid the door open. The outer air was deadly cold. The sun was a huge dull-red ball hanging in the haze of a grey sky. The rocks were grey-black, with the blood-light of the sun upon them.

Five hundred feet from us, by the shore of an oily, sullen sea, the wreckage of Tugh's cage was piled in a heap. Near it, the crumpled white figure of Mary lay on the rocks. And beside her, still with his black cloak around him, crouched Tugh!

CHAPTER TWENTY-THREE
Diabolical Exile of Time!

TUGH saw us as we stood in our cage doorway. His thick barrel-like figure rose erect, and from his parted cloak his arms waved with a wild gesture of defiance and triumph. He was clearly outlined in the red sunlight against the surface of the sea behind. We saw in one of his hands a ray cylinder—and then his arm came down and he fired at us. It was the white, disintegrating ray.

We were stricken by surprise, and stood for that moment transfixed in our doorway. Tugh's narrow, intensely white beam leaped over the intervening rocks; but it fell short of us. I saw that it had a range of about a hundred feet. Over the muffled heavy silence of the blood-red day the cripple's curse floated clear. He lowered his weapon; and, heedless that we also might be armed, he leaped nimbly past Mary's prostrate form and came shambling over the rocks directly for me!

It stung me into action, and for all the chaotic rush of these desperate moments my heart surged with relief. Mary was not dead! Beyond Tugh's oncoming figure, as he shambled like an infuriated charging bear over the rough rocky ground, I saw the white form of Mary move! She was striving to sit up!

I held my ray cylinder—the one I had rescued from Migul. But its range was no more than twenty feet: I had tested it; and Tugh's beam had flashed a full hundred! I whirled on Larry.

"Get away from here, you and Tina! You can't help me!"

"George, listen—"

"He's coming. Larry—you damn fool, get away from here! It goes a hundred feet, that ray of his: it'll be raking us in a minute! Run, I tell you! Get to that line of rocks!"

CLOSE behind our cage was a small broken ridge of rocks—strewn boulders in a tumbled line some ten or fifteen feet in height. It would afford shelter: there were broken places to give passage through it. The ridge curved crescent-shaped behind our cage and ran down toward the shore.

Larry and Tina stood white and confused. Larry panted, "But, George. I can help you fight him! Hide here in the cage—"

"Get away, I tell you! It's his death or mine this time! I'll get him if I can!"

I shoved Larry violently away and ducked back into our doorway. Only a few breathless seconds had passed; Tugh was still several hundred feet away from us. Larry and Tina ran behind the cage, darted between the boulders of the ridge and vanished.

I crouched in the cage. Tugh was not visible from here. A moment passed. Dared I remain? If I could get Tugh within twenty feet of me, my shot was as good as his... The silence was horrible. Was he coming forward? Did he know I was in here? I thought surely he must have seen Larry and Tina run away, and me dart in here: we had all been in plain sight of him.

This horrible silence! Was he creeping up on me? Would he fire through the doorway, or appear abruptly at the window? I could not tell where to place myself in the room—and it could mean my life or death.

The silence was split by Tina calling, "Tugh, we have caught you!"

HER voice was to one side and behind our cage, calling defiance at Tugh to distract his attention from me. Through the window I saw the flash of his beam, slanting sidewise at Tina. I gauged the source of his ray to be still some distance off, and crept to the door, cautiously peering.

Tugh stood on the open rock surface. He had swung to my right and was near the little ridge of rocks where it turned and bent down to the shore. Behind me came Tina's voice again:

"At last we have you, Tugh!"

I saw Tina poised on the top of the ridge, partially behind me at the elbow of the ridge-curve. She screamed her defiance, and again Tugh fired at her. The beam slanted over me, but still was short.

Larry had vanished. Then I saw him, though Tugh did not. He had run along behind the ridge, and appeared, now, well down toward the shore. He was barely a hundred feet from the cripple. I saw him stoop, seize a chunk of rock, and throw it. The missile bounded and passed close to Tugh.

Larry instantly ducked back out of sight. The bounding stone startled Tugh; he whirled toward it and fired over the ridge. Tina again had changed her position and was shouting at him. They were trying to exhaust his cylinder charges; and if they could do that he would be helpless before me.

FOR a moment he stood as though confused. As he turned to gaze after Tina, Larry flung another rock. But this time Tugh did not fire. He started back toward where, by the wreckage of his cage, Mary was now sitting up in a daze; then he changed his mind, whirled and fired directly at my doorway. I was just beyond the effective range of his beam, but it was truly aimed: I felt the horrible nauseous impact of it, a shuddering, indescribable sickening of all my being. I staggered back into the room and recovered my strength. A side window porte was open; I leaped through it and landed upon the rocks, with the cage between Tugh and me.

He fired again at the doorway. Tina had disappeared. Larry was now out of range, standing on the ridge, shouting and hurling rocks.

But Tugh did not heed him. He was shambling for my doorway. He would pass within twenty feet of me as I crouched outside the cage at its opposite corner. I could take him by surprise.

And then he saw me. He was less than a hundred feet away. He changed his direction and fired again, full at me. But I had had enough warning, and, as the beam struck the cage corner, I ran back along the outer wall of the cage and appeared at the other corner. Tugh came still closer, his weapon pointed downward as he ran. Fifty feet away. Not close enough!

I think, there at the last, that Tugh was wholly confused. Larry had come much closer. He was shouting: and from the ridge behind me Tina was shouting. Tugh ran, not for where I was lurking now, but for the corner where a moment before he had seen me.

Now he was thirty feet from me... Twenty... Then nearer than that. Wholly without caution he came forward... I leaned around the edge of the cage and fired. For one breathless instant the voices of Tina and Larry abruptly hushed.

My beam struck Tugh in the chest. It caught him and clung to him, bathing him in its spreading, intense white glare. He stopped in his tracks; stood transfixed for one breathless, horrible instant! He was so close that I could see the stupid surprise on his hideous features. His wide slit of mouth gaped with astonishment.

MY beam clung to him, but he did not fall! He stood astonished; then turned and came at me! For just a moment I was stricken helpless there before him. What manner of man was this? *He did not fall!* My ray, which had decomposed the body of Alent, the guard, and left his skeleton stripped and bleached in an instant, did not harm Tugh! He had walked into it, taken it full and he did not fall! He was still alive!

I came to my senses and saw that Larry, seeing my danger, had run into the open, dangerously close, and hurled a rock. It struck Tugh upon the shoulder and deflected his aim, so that his flash went over me. I saw Tugh whirl toward Larry, and I rushed forward, ripping loose the cylinder of the ray projector from its restraining battery cord. In the instant the cripple was turned half way from me I landed upon him, and with all my strength brought the point of the small heavy cylinder down on his skull. There was a strange splintering crack, and a wild, eery scream from his voice. He fell, with me on top of him.

Crowning horror! Tugh lay motionless, twisted half on his back, his thick arms outstretched on the rocks and his weapon still clutched in his hand. Culminating, gruesome horror! I rose from his body and stood shuddering. Amazing realization! The bulging misshapen head was splintered open. And from it, strewn over the rocks, were tiny intricate cogs and wheels, coils and broken wires!

He was not a man, but a Robot! A Super-Robot from some unknown era, running amuck! A mechanism so cleverly fashioned by the genius of man that it stood diabolically upon the threshhold of humanity!

A super-mechanical exile of Time! But its wild, irrational career of destruction through the ages now was over. It lay inert, smashed and broken at my feet...

CHAPTER TWENTY-FOUR
The Return

I THINK that there is little I should add. Tugh's last purpose had been to hurl himself and Mary past the lifetime of our world, wrecking the cage and flinging them into Eternity together. And Tugh was luring our cage and us to the same fate. But Mary, to save us, had watched her opportunity, seized the main control lever and demolished the vehicle by its instantaneous stopping.

We left the shell of Tugh lying there in the red sunlight of the empty, dying world, and returned to Tina's palace. We found that the revolt was over. The city, with help arrived, was striving to emerge from the bloody chaos. Larry and Tina decided to remain permanently in her Time. They would take us back; but the cage was too diabolical to keep in existence.

"I shall send it forward unoccupied," said Tina; "flash it into Eternity, where Tugh tried to go."

Accompanied by Larry, she carried Mary and me to 1935. With Mary's father, her only relative, dead, she yielded to my urging. We arrived in October, 1935. My New York, like Tina's a victim of the exile of Time, was rapidly being reconstructed.

IT was night when we stopped and the familiar outlines of Patton Place were around us.

We stood at the cage doorway.

"Good-by," I said to Larry and Tina. "Good luck to you both!"

The girls kissed each other. Such strangely contrasting types! Over a thousand years was between them, yet how alike they were, fundamentally. Both—just girls.

Larry gripped my hand. In times of emotion one is sometimes inarticulate. "Good-by, George," he said. "We— we've said already all there is to say, haven't we?"

There were tears in both the girls' eyes. We four had been so close; we had been through so much together; and now we were parting forever. All four of us were stricken with surprise at how it affected us. We stood gazing at one another.

"No!" I burst out. "I haven't said all there is to say. Don't you destroy that cage! You come back! Guard it as carefully as you can, and come back. Land here, next year in October; say, night of the 15th. Will you? We'll be here waiting."

"Yes," Tina abruptly agreed.

We stood watching them as they slid the door closed. The cage for a moment stood quiescent. Then it began faintly humming. It glowed; faded to a spectre; and was gone.

Mary and I turned away into the New York City of 1935, to begin our life together.

THE END

FOOTNOTES

[1] The workings of the Time-telespectroscope involve all the intricate postulates and mathematical formulae of Time-traveling itself. As a matter of practicality, however, the results obtained are simple of understanding. The etheric vibratory rate of the vehicles while traveling through Time was constantly changing. Through the telespectroscope one cage was visible to the other across the five hundred feet of intervening Space when they approached a simultaneous Time; when they, so to speak, were tuned in unison.

Thus, Harl explained, the other cage would show as a ghost, the faintest of wraiths, over a Time-distance of some five or ten years. And the closer in Time they approached it, the more solid it would appear.

[2] At the risk of repetition I must make the following clear: Time-traveling only consumes Time in the sense of the perception of human consciousness that the trip has duration. The vehicles thus moved "fast" or "slow" according to the rate of change which the controls of the cage gave its inherent vibration factors. Too sudden a change could not be withstood by the human passengers. Hence the trips—for them—had duration.

Migul took Mary and me from 1935 to 1777. The flight seems perhaps half an hour. At a greater rate of vibration change, we sped to 2930; and back and forth from 2930 to 1935. At each successive arrival in 1935, Migul so skilfully calculated the stop that it occurred upon the same night, at the same hour, and only a minute or so later. And in 2930 he achieved the same result. To one who might stand at either end and watch the cage depart, the round trip was made in three or four minutes at most.

[3] Upon a later calculation I judged that the average passage of the years in relation to my perception of Time-rate was slightly over 277,500 years a second. Undoubtedly throughout the myriad centuries preceding the birth of mankind our rate was very considerably faster than that; and from the dawn of history forward—which is so tiny a fraction of the whole—we traveled materially slower.

[4] In 2930, all aircraft engines were operated by radio-power transmitted by senders in various districts. The New York Power House controlled a local district of about two hundred miles radius.

[5] Cylinder records of books which by machinery gave audible rendition, in similar fashion to the radio-phonograph.

[6] The Power House on the Hudson dam was operated by inert machinery and manned entirely by humans—the only place in the city which was so handled. This was because of its extreme importance. The air-power was broadcast from there. Without that power the entire several hundred mile district around New York would be dead. No aircraft could enter, save perhaps some skilfully handled motorless glider, if aided by sufficiently fortuitous air currents. Every surface vehicle used this power, and every sub-sea freighter. The city lights, and every form of city power, were centralized here also, as well as the broadcasting audible and etheric transmitters and receivers. Without the Power House, New York City and all its neighborhood would be inoperative, and cut off from the outside world.

[7] I mentioned the small conning tower on top of the laboratory building and the Robot lookout there with his audible broadcasting.

[8] This was part of Tugh's plan. The broadcast voice was the signal for the uprising in the New York district. This tower broadcaster could only reach the local area, yet ships and land vehicles with Robot operators would doubtless pick it up and relay it further. The mechanical revolt would spread. And on the ships, the airliners and the land vehicles, the Robot operators stirred to sudden frenzy would run amuck. As a matter of fact, there were indeed many accidents to ships and vehicles this night when their operators abruptly went beyond control. The chaos ran around the world like a fire in prairie grass.

[9] The police army had one weapon: a small vibration hand-ray. Its vibrating current beam could, at a distance of ten or twenty feet, reduce a Robot into paralyzed subjection; or, with more intense vibration, burn out the Robot's coils and fuses.

[10] The storage batteries by which the Robot actuating energy was renewed, and the fuses, coils and other appliances necessary to the Robot existence, were all guarded now in the Power House.

[11] As a matter of actuality, Tugh was carrying hidden upon his person a small cylinder and battery of the deadly white-ray. It seems probable that although on the catwalk—having accomplished his purpose of getting within the electrical fortifications of the dam—Tugh had ample opportunity of killing his over-trustful companions with the white-ray, he did not dare use it. The catwalk was too dark

for their figures to be visible to the Power House guards; the roar of the spillways drowned their shouts; but had Tugh used the white-ray, its abnormally intense actinic white beam would have raised the alarm which Tugh most of all wanted to avoid.

[12] It will be recalled that Tugh passed Alent's gate, and with Tina and Larry went to the palace roof. Perhaps, while Larry was with the Council during that time when the Robot revolt was first sweeping over the city, Tugh may again have prowled down here in these lower corridors. Then he went upstairs, brought Tina and Larry down and they started for the Power House.

[13] Had Migul at that juncture traced Tina's movements—her hand where it went along the tunnel-wall—we would have found the light switch. But it chanced that the Robot's fingers went at once to the ground and caught the foot-trail of Tugh.

[14] The cylinder of the white-ray which I carried was not the one with which Tugh murdered Harl. Mine was portable, and considerably smaller.

[15] Tugh had been in the Power House before. He knew the operations of its various controls. But he had come always by the surface route; he had heard of the existence of the secret tunnel, but had never before this night been able to find out where it was.

[16] There was a similar gate and wall-barrier at the Jersey entrance to the dam, and both gates operated together. The nearby Jersey section was, is still, an agricultural district save for a few landing stages for the great airliners. The robots

had spread into Jersey; but since few humans were there, with only Robot agriculturists working the section, the unimportant Jersey events have not figured in my narrative.

[17] It was afterward found that many of the Robots, heedless of the rain as they ran about the city intent upon their murderous work, had exploded by getting too wet.

If you've enjoyed this book, you will not want to miss these terrific titles…

ARMCHAIR SCI-FI & HORROR DOUBLE NOVELS, $12.95 each

D-51 **A GOD NAMED SMITH** by Henry Slesar
WORLDS OF THE IMPERIUM by Keith Laumer

D-52 **CRAIG'S BOOK** by Don Wilcox
EDGE OF THE KNIFE by H. Beam Piper

D-53 **THE SHINING CITY** by Rena M. Vale
THE RED PLANET by Russ Winterbotham

D-54 **THE MAN WHO LIVED TWICE** by Rog Phillips
VALLEY OF THE CROEN by Lee Tarbell

D-55 **OPERATION DISASTER** by Milton Lesser
LAND OF THE DAMNED by Berkeley Livingston

D-56 **CAPTIVE OF THE CENTAURIANESS** by Poul Anderson
A PRINCESS OF MARS by Edgar Rice Burroughs

D-57 **THE NON-STATISTICAL MAN** by Raymond F. Jones
MISSION FROM MARS by Rick Conroy

D-58 **INTRUDERS FROM THE STARS** by Ross Rocklynne
FLIGHT OF THE STARLING by Chester S. Geier

D-59 **COSMIC SABOTEUR** by Frank M. Robinson
LOOK TO THE STARS by Willard Hawkins

D-60 **THE MOON IS HELL!** by John W. Campbell, Jr.
THE GREEN WORLD by Hal Clement

ARMCHAIR SCIENCE FICTION CLASSICS, $12.95 each

C-16 **THE SHAVER MYSTERY, Book Three**
by Richard S. Shaver

C-17 **THE PLANET STRAPPERS**
by Raymond Z. Gallun

C-18 **THE FOURTH "R"**
by George O. Smith

ARMCHAIR SCI-FI & HORROR GEMS SERIES, $12.95 each

G-5 **SCIENCE FICTION GEMS, Vol. Three**
C. M. Kornbluth and others

G-6 **HORROR GEMS, Vol. Three**
August Derleth and others

If you've enjoyed this book, you will not want to miss these terrific titles…

ARMCHAIR SCI-FI & HORROR DOUBLE NOVELS, $12.95 each

D-61 **THE MAN WHO STOPPED AT NOTHING** by Paul W. Fairman
TEN FROM INFINITY by Ivar Jorgensen

D-62 **WORLDS WITHIN** by Rog Phillips
THE SLAVE by C.M. Kornbluth

D-63 **SECRET OF THE BLACK PLANET** by Milton Lesser
THE OUTCASTS OF SOLAR III by Emmett McDowell

D-64 **WEB OF THE WORLDS** by Harry Harrison and Katherine MacLean
RULE GOLDEN by Damon Knight

D-65 **TEN TO THE STARS** by Raymond Z. Gallun
THE CONQUERORS by David H. Keller, M. D.

D-66 **THE HORDE FROM INFINITY** by Dwight V. Swain
THE DAY THE EARTH FROZE by Gerald Hatch

D-67 **THE WAR OF THE WORLDS** by H. G. Wells
THE TIME MACHINE by H. G. Wells

D-68 **STARCOMBERS** by Edmond Hamilton
THE YEAR WHEN STARDUST FELL by Raymond F. Jones

D-69 **HOCUS-POCUS UNIVERSE** by Jack Williamson
QUEEN OF THE PANTHER WORLD by Berkeley Livingston

D-70 **BATTERING RAMS OF SPACE** by Don Wilcox
DOOMSDAY WING by George H. Smith

ARMCHAIR SCIENCE FICTION CLASSICS, $12.95 each

C-19 **EMPIRE OF JEGGA**
by David V. Reed

C-20 **THE TOMORROW PEOPLE**
by Judith Merril

C-21 **THE MAN FROM YESTERDAY**
by Howard Browne as by Lee Francis

C-22 **THE TIME TRADERS**
by Andre Norton

C-23 **ISLANDS OF SPACE**
by John W. Campbell

C-24 **THE GALAXY PRIMES**
by E. E. "Doc" Smith

If you've enjoyed this book, you will not want to miss these terrific titles...

ARMCHAIR SCI-FI & HORROR DOUBLE NOVELS, $12.95 each

D-71   **THE DEEP END** by Gregory Luce
TO WATCH BY NIGHT by Robert Moore Williams

D-72   **SWORDSMAN OF LOST TERRA** by Poul Anderson
PLANET OF GHOSTS by David V. Reed

D-73   **MOON OF BATTLE** by J. J. Allerton
THE MUTANT WEAPON by Murray Leinster

D-74   **OLD SPACEMEN NEVER DIE!** John Jakes
RETURN TO EARTH by Bryan Berry

D-75   **THE THING FROM UNDERNEATH** by Milton Lesser
OPERATION INTERSTELLAR by George O. Smith

D-76   **THE BURNING WORLD** by Algis Budrys
FOREVER IS TOO LONG by Chester S. Geier

D-77   **THE COSMIC JUNKMAN** by Rog Phillips
THE ULTIMATE WEAPON by John W. Campbell

D-78   **THE TIES OF EARTH** by James H. Schmitz
CUE FOR QUIET by Thomas L. Sherred

D-79   **SECRET OF THE MARTIANS** by Paul W. Fairman
THE VARIABLE MAN by Philip K. Dick

D-80   **THE GREEN GIRL** by Jack Williamson
THE ROBOT PERIL by Don Wilcox

ARMCHAIR SCIENCE FICTION CLASSICS, $12.95 each

C-25   **THE STAR KINGS**
b   y Edmond Hamilton

C-26   **NOT IN SOLITUDE**
by Kenneth Gantz

C-32   **PROMETHEUS II**
by S. J. Byrne

ARMCHAIR SCI-FI & HORROR GEMS SERIES, $12.95 each

G-7   **SCIENCE FICTION GEMS, Vol. Four**
Jack Sharkey and others

G-8   **HORROR GEMS, Vol. Four**
Seabury Quinn and others

If you've enjoyed this book, you will not want to miss these terrific titles…

ARMCHAIR SCI-FI & HORROR DOUBLE NOVELS, $12.95 each

D-81   **THE LAST PLEA** by Robert Bloch
THE STATUS CIVILIZATION by Robert Sheckley

D-82   **WOMAN FROM ANOTHER PLANET** by Frank Belknap Long
HOMECALLING by Judith Merril

D-83   **WHEN TWO WORLDS MEET** by Robert Moore Williams
THE MAN WHO HAD NO BRAINS by Jeff Sutton

D-84   **THE SPECTRE OF SUICIDE SWAMP** by E. K. Jarvis
IT'S MAGIC, YOU DOPE! by Jack Sharkey

D-85   **THE STARSHIP FROM SIRIUS** by Rog Phillips
FINAL WEAPON by Everett Cole

D-86   **TREASURE ON THUNDER MOON** by Edmond Hamilton
TRAIL OF THE ASTROGAR by Henry Haase

D-87   **THE VENUS ENIGMA** by Joe Gibson
THE WOMAN IN SKIN 13 by Paul W. Fairman

D-88   **THE MAD ROBOT** by William P. McGivern
THE RUNNING MAN by J. Holly Hunter

D-89   **VENGEANCE OF KYVOR** by Randall Garrett
AT THE EARTH'S CORE by Edgar Rice Burroughs

D-90   **DWELLERS OF THE DEEP** by Don Wilcox
NIGHT OF THE LONG KNIVES by Fritz Leiber

ARMCHAIR SCIENCE FICTION CLASSICS, $12.95 each

C-28   **THE MAN FROM TOMORROW**
by Stanton A. Coblentz

C-29   **THE GREEN MAN OF GRAYPEC**
by Festus Pragnell

C-30   **THE SHAVER MYSTERY, Book Four**
by Richard S. Shaver

ARMCHAIR MASTERS OF SCIENCE FICTION SERIES, $16.95 each

MS-7   **MASTERS OF SCIENCE FICTION AND FANTASY, Vol. Seven**
Lester del Rey, "The Band Played On" and other tales

MS-8   **MASTERS OF SCIENCE FICTION, Vol. Eight**
Milton Lesser, "'A' as in Android" and other tales

If you've enjoyed this book, you will not want to miss these terrific titles…

ARMCHAIR SCI-FI & HORROR DOUBLE NOVELS, $12.95 each

D-91 **THE TIME TRAP** by Henry Kuttner
THE LUNAR LICHEN by Hal Clement

D-92 **SARGASSO OF LOST STARSHIPS** by Poul Anderson
THE ICE QUEEN by Don Wilcox

D-93 **THE PRINCE OF SPACE** by Jack Williamson
POWER by Harl Vincent

D-94 **PLANET OF NO RETURN** by Howard Browne
THE ANNIHILATOR COMES by Ed Earl Repp

D-95 **THE SINISTER INVASION** by Edmond Hamilton
OPERATION TERROR by Murray Leinster

D-96 **TRANSIENT** by Ward Moore
THE WORLD-MOVER by George O. Smith

D-97 **FORTY DAYS HAS SEPTEMBER** by Milton Lesser
THE DEVIL'S PLANET by David Wright O'Brien

D-98 **THE CYBERENE** by Rog Phillips
BADGE OF INFAMY by Lester del Rey

D-99 **THE JUSTICE OF MARTIN BRAND** by Raymond A. Palmer
BRING BACK MY BRAIN by Dwight V. Swain

D-100 **WIDE-OPEN PLANET** by L. Sprague de Camp
AND THEN THE TOWN TOOK OFF by Richard Wilson

ARMCHAIR SCIENCE FICTION CLASSICS, $12.95 each

C-31 **THE GOLDEN GUARDSMEN**
by S. J. Byrne

C-32 **ONE AGAINST THE MOON**
by Donald A. Wollheim

C-33 **HIDDEN CITY**
by Chester S. Geier

ARMCHAIR SCI-FI & HORROR GEMS SERIES, $12.95 each

G-9 **SCIENCE FICTION GEMS, Vol. Five**
Clifford D. Simak and others

G-10 **HORROR GEMS, Vol. Five**
E. Hoffman Price and others

If you've enjoyed this book, you will not want to miss these terrific titles…

ARMCHAIR SCI-FI & HORROR DOUBLE NOVELS, $12.95 each

D-101 **THE CONQUEST OF THE PLANETS** by John W. Campbell
THE MAN WHO ANNEXED THE MOON by Bob Olsen

D-102 **WEAPON FROM THE STARS** by Rog Phillips
THE EARTH WAR by Mack Reynolds

D-103 **THE ALIEN INTELLIGENCE** by Jack Williamson
INTO THE FOURTH DIMENSION by Ray Cummings

D-104 **THE CRYSTAL PLANETOIDS** by Stanton A. Coblentz
SURVIVORS FROM 9,000 B. C. by Robert Moore Williams

D-105 **THE TIME PROJECTOR** by David H. Keller, M.D. and David Lasser
STRANGE COMPULSION by Philip Jose Farmer

D-106 **WHOM THE GODS WOULD SLAY** by Paul W. Fairman
MEN IN THE WALLS by William Tenn

D-107 **LOCKED WORLDS** by Edmond Hamilton
THE LAND THAT TIME FORGOT by Edgar Rice Burroughs

D-108 **STAY OUT OF SPACE** by Dwight V. Swain
REBELS OF THE RED PLANET by Charles L. Fontenay

D-109 **THE METAMORPHS** by S. J. Byrne
MICROCOSMIC BUCCANEERS by Harl Vincent

D-110 **YOU CAN'T ESCAPE FROM MARS** by E. K. Jarvis
THE MAN WITH FIVE LIVES by David V. Reed

ARMCHAIR SCIENCE FICTION CLASSICS, $12.95 each

C-34 **30 DAY WONDER**
by Richard Wilson

C-35 **G.O.G. 666**
by John Taine

C-36 **RALPH 124C 41+**
by Hugo Gernsback

ARMCHAIR SCI-FI & HORROR GEMS SERIES, $12.95 each

G-11 **SCIENCE FICTION GEMS, Vol. Six**
Edmond Hamilton and others

G-12 **HORROR GEMS, Vol. Six**
H. P. Lovecraft and others

If you've enjoyed this book, you will not want to miss these terrific titles…

ARMCHAIR SCI-FI & HORROR DOUBLE NOVELS, $12.95 each

D-111   **THE MOON ERA** by Jack Williamson
            REVENGE OF THE ROBOTS by Howard Browne

D-112   **SON OF THE BLACK CHALICE** by Milton Lesser
            SENTRY OF THE SKY by Evelyn E. Smith

D-113   **OUTPOST ON THE MOON** by Joslyn Maxwell
            POTENTIAL ZERO by S. J. Byrne

D-114   **OUTPOST INFINITY** by Raymond F. Jones
            THE WHITE INVADERS by Ray Cummings

D-115   **TIME TRAP** by Rog Phillips
            THE COSMIC DESTROYER by Alexander Blade

D-116   **THE OTHER SIDE OF THE MOON** by Edmond Hamilton
            SECRET INVASION by Walter Kubilius

D-117   **DANGER MOON** by Frederik Pohl
            THE HIDDEN UNIVERSE by Ralph Milne Farley

D-118   **THE WAILING ASTEROID** by Murray Leinster
            THE WORLD THAT COULDN'T BE by Clifford D. Simak

D-119   **THE WHISPERING GORILLA** by Don Wilcox
            RETURN OF THE WHISPERING GORILLA by David V. Reed

D-120   **SPECIAL EFFECT** by J. F. Bone
            WARLORD OF KOR by Terry Carr

ARMCHAIR SCIENCE FICTION CLASSICS, $12.95 each

C-37   **THE GREEN MAN RETURNS**
           by Harold M. Sherman

C-38   **THE SHAVER MYSTERY, Book Five**
           by Richard S, Shaver

C-39   **MARS CHILD**
           by Cyril Judd

ARMCHAIR MASTERS OF SCIENCE FICTION SERIES, $16.95 each

MS-9   **MASTERS OF SCIENCE FICTION AND FANTASY, Vol. Nine**
            Poul Anderson, "The Star Beast" and other tales

MS-10   **MASTERS OF SCIENCE FICTION, Vol. Ten**
            Robert Moore Williams, "Time Tolls for Toro" and other tales

If you've enjoyed this book, you will not want to miss these terrific titles…

ARMCHAIR MYSTERY & SCIENCE FICTION CLASSICS
$12.95 each

C-40 **MODEL FOR MURDER**
by Stephen Marlowe

C-41 **PRELUDE TO MURDER**
by Sterling Noel

C-42 **DEAD WEIGHT**
by Frank Kane

C-43 **A DAME CALLED MURDER**
by Milton Ozaki

C-44 **THE GREATEST ADVENTURE**
by John Taine

C-45 **THE EXILE OF TIME**
by Ray Cummings

C-46 **STORM OVER WARLOCK**
by Andre Norton

C-47 **MAN OF MANY MINDS**
by E. Everett Evans

C-48 **THE GODS OF MARS**
by Edgar Rice Burroughs

C-49 **BRIGANDS OF THE MOON**
by Ray Cummings

C-50 **SPACE HOUNDS OF IPC**
by E. E. "Doc" Smith

C-51 **THE LANI PEOPLE**
by J. F. Bone

C-52 **THE MOON POOL**
by A. Merritt

C-53 **IN THE DAYS OF THE COMET**
by H. G. Wells

C-55 **TRIPLANETARY**
E. E. "Doc" Smith